A. V. DALCOURT

AWAKENING FRACTURED MEMORIES
VOLUME 1

ಸ   A DARK FANTASY SHORT STORY COLLECTION   ಲ

in association with
FANTASY ETHOS

First Fantasy Ethos paperback edition May 2021

Names: Dalcourt, A. V., author
Title: Awakening Fractured Memories Volume 1 / A. V. Dalcourt
Description: First edition. | Sudbury : Fantasy Ethos, 2021. | Series: Awakening Fractured Memories ; Book 1
Identifiers: ISBN (paperback) 9780987902795
Subjects: BISAC: FICTION / Fantasy / Supernatural. | FICTION / Fantasy / Adventure. | GSAFD: Fantasy

ISBNs: (ebook) 9780987902771;
ISBNs: (paperback) 9780987902795;

DEDICATION TO MY FATHER
who insisted I should write

‽℈

BY A. V. DALCOURT

AWAKENING FRACTURED MEMORIES SHORT FICTION
Dream Eater
The Game: Beta Testing

AWAKENING FRACTURED MEMORIES COLLECTION
Awakening Fractured Memories: Volume 1

AWAKENING: PRODIGY
Book 1: Hunter's Gambit - coming soon -
Book 2: Ghost in the Machine - coming soon -
Book 3: Hunter's Game - coming soon -
Book 4: Ascension - coming soon -

STORIES

PREFACE

Awakening Fractured Memories is a series of short stories set in alternate universes to the Awakening series. Featured characters and scenarios may or may not have played a role in the current Awakening stories. These short stories give readers more time with the characters and in the world in which they exist. Each short story is intended to represent a moment in an alternate version of the timeline. Details, subtle or obvious, may deviate from one story to the next. This is not a continuity error. This is intentional. The 'Fractured Memories' are meant to be half-remembered stories as told from the perspective of a chosen character. Not a single one of the characters is intended to be a 100% reliable narrator. Readers may have diverse opinions when piecing the story together as they interpret the narratives of the characters. Continuity or a through-line involving a larger story tying in all of the short stories is purely coincidental.

The Fractured Memories stories are add-ons to Awakening which is, as of this writing, in its third draft stage. You can keep an eye out for progress reports on the Awakening website over at: www.AwakeningAnthology.com

I base most of the short stories on a series of dreams recorded in a dream journal that later shape the world and characters of the Awakening. The few stories whose plots don't stem from the dream journals are exercises in exploring and developing characters and ideas that stem from the main work of the Awakening series, or reader requests.

I base Dream Eater on a few lines scribbled in my dream journal when I was thirteen years old. All I had to work with was an abandoned old garage with a potted plant sitting in a broken window. Through the broken window a shaft of light touched a portion of the plant. In its light, was a healthy plant with small moons ready to pick. On the shaded side of the plant, they were wilted, barren, dying.

This is the seed of the idea that led to Dream Eater.

The Game: Beta Testing is based on a few lines jotted down in my dream journal. A school play production is broadcast to the nation. An overly dramatic lead actress swoons: "Take me to my father and you will be handsomely rewarded." The hero hesitates.

The Game: Beta Testing is the start of the development of what later becomes the Ghost in the Machine arc of Awakening: Prodigy.

Arcanum Mutatios' inception, like The Game: Beta Testing, left a lot of wiggle room for interpretation. I set the story through William's perspective because, as one of the primary trio for Awakening: Prodigy, I had yet to get properly acquainted with his character and voice. Like the aforementioned short story, I had only a line to work with. 'I was a flea, a blind, winged creature soaring through the sky, and a monster.' Reading back over the line years later, I have a vivid recollection of struggling to maintain lucidity in the various forms. As an adult, I recognize the science as I understand it. My R.E.M. cycle was being interrupted, but I was falling back asleep just as fast as I was disturbed. My mind melded snippets of memories: a documentary, lore from the mythology I was studying in high school, and an irritating seasonal problem we were enduring with our pets. I love how our minds process our daily lives, transforming the mundane into something fantastical.

Guiding Light is based on a dream that centered on an old book (at that age I was deeply interested in prophecies), a rapidly disintegrating reality, and chaotic battle between unknown factions monstrous, human, and occult; all while the protagonist tried to protect the book. This is not the story I tell with Guiding Light, but it is something like it.

Shadow Prey Part I was a challenge to decide on which story to tell and on how to write it. I discovered that I could craft many stories with the same key elements. The latter part of the dream, in my humble opinion, was far more interesting than the beginning portion. Shadow Prey was also my first commitment to writing short fiction from beginning to the end, just to see if I could manage it. It was a small relief to learn that yes, I can finish a writing project... even if it takes me three months to be satisfied with eight thousand words.

Finally, we have Shadow Prey Part II which is a response to my beta readers who complained (and rightfully so) that there was no satisfying ending to Shadow Prey Part I. In my defense, Shadow Prey Part I was an experiment in so many ways. It was an effort to see if I could maintain the interest in a piece long enough to complete it. It was permission to try out another writer's advice and method for a restricted (but not too restricted) word count. It was my permission to practice becoming a better storyteller. I never expected it to hit best seller status. I never expected to have readers ask if they could write the ending. I never expected it to go anywhere. It just was.

Unlike the previous short stories, Shadow Prey Part II doesn't follow any dreams. I am a writer after all, and at the time I felt that I should be able to come up with a plausible story that could stand on its own. Six months and far too many re-writes later, I finished it.

Awakening fans! Here's part II! Enjoy my suffering!

DREAM EATER

DREAM EATER

Daamon manor had returned to its former glory. The core three-storey household had been resurrected. Manicured gardens replaced the burnt wreckage of its massive wings. The vast open grounds and isolated location were ideal for the councilman's plans for his granddaughter, to give her the space she needed to train as a Demon Hunter.

A black car broke through the wooded drive and pulled to a stop in front of the main doors. Philip, the councilman's bodyguard who doubled as his chauffeur, was an imposing bald man in a neat black suit, which was too expensive for his station. He got out, opened his master's door, and waited with one arm posed behind his back as he stared straight ahead.

The councilman, Dezmond Daamon, a well-dressed older gentleman, glanced up from his reports, blinded by the light. "Hold on," he bade the holographic image of his eldest son, Damien. The miniature version of Damien stood on a thin sheet that was set on top of the center console of the backseat. Dezmond appeared to be a modern-day wizard and was fast approaching his senior years. His hair had been grey the day Damien was born to him, but had only recently begun to recede. He was thankful, in some respects, that the recession was gradual and would not grace him with a horseshoe hairline. Instead, it emphasized his widow's peak.

The public nature of his work required him to keep his hair short and his beard well groomed. In his youth, he had once fancied a beard much like the great wizard Gandalf, of the *Lord of the Rings* books that he had read with his older brother Alistair.

"Pops," Damien said, "I'm in the process of calibrating the demon defence systems. When the shields go up, it'll keep the demons out, but if there's anything still wandering around that house, it'll be stuck in there with you." Damien paused only ever so slightly, before switching to the topic he preferred. "At least it'll be a contained area to test the legend against the real deal… Could be that our ancestors may have blown the stories a little out of proportion over the millennia."

Damien was a successful middle-aged businessman and engineer. He had trimmed his mustache and goatee in the current fashion, but on most days, he was in a disheveled state, giving him the aura of a man who had exhausted his empathy and ambition. Today, he had combed back his dark hair, though his wild grey eyes still betrayed his insanity.

"Have faith," Dezmond murmured, struck by the appearance of his former family home.

Damien narrowed his eyes as his father stepped out of the car. "I can tell that this is going nowhere," he shouted after the old man. "I'll just do what I need to do and save your senile old ass, as always!"

"You do that," Dezmond replied, signalling the transmission to end. He slid the projection screen closed, folding his tablet to a small cylinder the size of a pen, and slid it into his inside coat pocket.

The manor looked exactly as he remembered, wiped clean of the tragedy that had befallen his family some twenty years ago. His heart beat against his chest, begging for an impossible chance to reunite with his late wife and daughter.

As he placed his hand on the metal handle of the front door, the cold bit him, like the sting of his reality. He took in a deep breath, steeling his mind against what he knew to be true. There was no one waiting to greet him. The house was empty.

He pushed the heavy entrance door open. The sounds of the real world fell away, replaced the desperate longing of children's playful squeals. He wished that the echoes of his distant past were real.

"I'm home." His voice was hoarse. He wiped the wet from his face. "It's okay to grieve," he told himself. "Just not right now."

Dezmond's fingers danced across the polished surface of the small, round table that sat in the middle of the entryway. Yellow flowers sat in a stout vase, filling the room with a scent that he had once despised. The petals came loose at his soft touch. He didn't recall hiring an agency to furnish the home.

Without warning, the ceiling came down on him, smashing him into the ground. He groaned against the pain, knowing that something had penetrated his back, and struggled to push himself onto all fours but the weight of the ceiling was too much to withstand. He clawed at the floor, hoping to find purchase. A massive black claw wrapped around the old man's head with care, forcing his face into the ground.

This was it, he would die at the hands of the demon that had consumed his family.

As his consciousness faded, he noticed two things. The first was the blood pooling from him, filling the room, and the second was the sound of Desdaria's voice calling to him.

"Dezmond..."

ଐଓଔ

"Dezmond!" A young boy pushed against him, urging him to wake.

Dezmond groaned. "Leave me alone."

The boy climbed up on him and pried his eyelids open. "I know you're awake, Dez. You promised you'd help me with my project! Now wake up! Waaaaaaake up."

They were in his childhood home, in the bedroom where he and Alistair had built forts out of their beds, using their blankets and pillows. One tall window allowed the moonlight to shine down on them.

Dezmond attempted to frown at Alistair, but it was far too difficult a feat when both top eyelids had been pulled from their respective eyes. "Get off, my eyeballs are shrivelling!" He pushed his sibling to the floor. "I thought you meant you wanted help tomorrow. It's got to be..." Dezmond reached for his digital clock and stared at the dark red numbers shining up at him. It took a moment for him to understand what he was reading; the numbers didn't quite make sense. His brain assured him that they said it was "far too early in the morning to be checking the time". He agreed with his brain and he put the clock down.

The boy smiled at him. Alistair was nine years old, Dezmond's elder brother and favourite playmate.

Dezmond remembered this night. It was August, and Alistair was eager to grow his own special berries this year. The concept of growing produce still eluded the children, but try they did, every year, by planting everything from buttons to sticks and watching and waiting for signs of growth.

Dezmond wasn't so keen on sneaking off to the shed to check on the progress of whatever Alistair had planted. He stared down at his older brother. He would find Alistair in the morning...

As if on cue, Alistair leaped to his feet and pulled on his brother's sleeve, playing out the memory, oblivious to the drastic change in Dezmond's age. "Come on! We don't know when Mom and Dad will be up!"

The older man got up out of his childhood bed, rubbing his back. His bones ached, and it hurt to breathe. He struggled to focus. Memories of a forgotten life nagged at him, begging for attention. Yet he couldn't grab hold of the threads of that reality. A part of him was desperate to remain with his brother, to return to a simpler time in his life. To a time where fighting demons was kept secret.

He followed Alistair out of their shared bedroom.

Giggling caught his attention. "You can't find me," came the familiar taunt of his young wife.

Dezmond's heart skipped a beat. He dashed deeper into the darkness of the corridor, leaving Alistair calling after him.

He was outside. The sunlight sparkled through the whispering leaves. It was late summer and his love for Desdaria was in full flux. He caught sight of her summer dress floating on a breeze, betraying her presence behind an ancient oak. He played along.

"One more hint," he called, a broad smile sneaking its way into his voice as he crept up on the tree.

"I've given you enough hints!" Desdaria said. He rushed up behind her, grabbing her into his arms and spun her around. She screamed with excitement. It felt good to hold her again. He never wanted to let her go.

Desdaria was the most beautiful creature he had ever seen.

She had long auburn hair, warm brown eyes, and a smile that could light up a room, especially when she smiled at him. She was of a thin build and shorter than average by a few noticeable inches. She had narrow hips, an aspect that the Military Regime considered a fault, as she did not have the acceptable build of a breeder. Her breasts were small, too, but she had wide shoulders and strong arms, shaped by her long hours tending to the family farm.

She kissed him, her love igniting a part of him he had thought dormant.

She pulled away. "Is it true that you're buying Daddy's land?"

"I am," Dezmond said truthfully. He didn't want to treat her as her father had treated her mother; he saw her as an equal, even though the Regime saw her as little more than livestock for breeding. They sat down on the hill overlooking her father's land. She leaned against him, listening to the sound of his voice.

"Your father is being pressured to give up his property, and I'm afraid for your safety and your family's if we don't do something soon. The people he's dealing with aren't scared to use acts of terrorism to get their way. So this morning I asked him to include the property as part of your dowry."

He felt her body tense. He added, "It's a formality. You see, your father can't sell the property outright unless the buyer has the approval of the

Regime. Which I do not. I am not as glorious or as honoured as they feel that I should be. But," he raised a finger and smiled at her, "he can include it as a wedding gift. You know, along with the three cows and seven sheep that he gave me to take you off of his hands," he said.

She slapped his arm as a rebuttal, but he pulled her in close. "Not only do I have a stronger standing in the community than your father, but as your landlord, a portion of the food produced here will be mine to claim," he said. "I've survived off of food cubes for a very long time, my dear. I haven't any problem returning the food to feed your family."

"You're doing this for us?" This confused her. Two of her older sisters had married well and ignored the family. She vowed to be different and made sure that Dezmond understood that she intended to care for her family. But some part of her had still doubted that her chosen husband would allow it.

"Given your father's condition and everything that's been going on, it'll be a long time before he will be treated with any respect," Dezmond said. "This is the only way that I could think of to avoid having him bullied off of his own property, or have your family starved out."

She sighed, taking this all in. "He had to have his arm replaced," she told him. The acquisition of a robotic part, no matter how necessary the piece, was viewed as unclean and unnatural. "What was he supposed to do?" Her father still needed to tend the farm. Failure to maintain food quotas for the region would rob the family of three generations of history.

"We'll be married in September," he said. "If you're not comfortable with... um... the arrangements, I'll be happy to wait until you're ready."

She blushed. He was older than she was by almost fifteen years, and her sisters had shared every gory detail of what transpired on their much-anticipated wedding nights, shocking her into fear. While not an uncommon arrangement, as her sisters both married men in their late fifties, she had always thought it unnatural and perverted for an old man to marry a child.

"You could have married me when I was sixteen," she told him, as she was just leaving her teen years now. Her statement was a test of his character and a form of reassurance. She hadn't consented to the marriage at first, but he didn't need her consent. She wanted to be sure that she wasn't marrying a monster. "I'm glad I didn't," Dezmond replied. "We wouldn't have had this opportunity otherwise."

He stroked her hair and held her tight. He had taken the time to nurture her love of him, and he would work every day to prove his love to her. He hoped that despite the way things ended, she knew that he loved her.

The shape of a child scurried past the house in the distance, looking for something, or perhaps someone. Dezmond watched him for some time. "I have to go," he told his young fiancée, "I promised to help with something back at the house."

He kissed her and promised to come back soon.

₧₨

As he moved down the steep hill toward the farmhouse, the day turned into night and his surroundings faded and shifted as his memory tried to work out the details. It was a warm night, befitting the season. Crickets sang, and the twilight twinkled in a variety of brilliant hues of yellows and blues, like some painted masterpiece he had seen somewhere before. He was in the backyard of his childhood home in the suburbs, a sleepy little community where everybody knew everybody's name. It was a time when humans were numerous and the biggest concern was freedom of speech. Government conspiracies were reserved for the paranoid.

As a child, the backyard had seemed massive and, because that was the way he remembered it, that's the way it appeared to him now. In the back of the property, there was an old workshop where his father used to fix machines of all kinds for the townsfolk, while his mother had a little area of her own for gardening tools.

Alistair had given up on waiting for Dezmond, just as he had all those years ago. Guilt ate at the old man. Had he been there, maybe he could have saved his brother. He followed the boy into the workshop.

Moonlight shone through the large, crooked window that resembled something out of a child's drawing. Rough concrete floors ran throughout the small workshop, evidence of the inexperienced and cheap labour that went into the construction of the old building.

Needing only a small space to slip through, and mindful of how loud the workshop door could sing in the quiet of the night, Dezmond ducked inside and allowed the door to lurch shut behind him, as though it was returning to its preferred sleeping position.

By the window, Alistair was logging his results in a journal. He had set up a terracotta pot with his mother's help and, like every year prior, had planted something to grow. Unlike their usual routine of checking in every day for about a week and then forgetting about it, the young boy had become obsessed with this year's project.

Metal crashed into the ground as something spooked and skittered, and Alistair looked up. "Dez, you came!"

"Yes," the old man said, "I promised to help." He approached the boy and his creation. The pot remained empty, save for the rich, dark dirt that filled it.

Alistair glanced over at their father's restoration project, a 1934 Mercedes-Benz Roadster, elevated on concrete blocks behind them. He frowned. "It's here again," he told Dezmond. "It's been trying to eat my plant. That's why we needed to come at night. To stop it from wrecking it!"

The old man regarded the empty pot before trying to catch a glimpse of the animal that Alistair referred to. The shadows cast by the moonlight made seeing shapes easy. If it were a living thing, its eyes would reflect the light, giving away its presence. He saw nothing. He heard nothing. It reminded him of searching for monsters under his children's beds.

"I thought with you here it would leave me alone. I guess I was wrong," Alistair said with a shrug and returned to his project journal.

Dezmond gave the space beneath the car a careful look before daring to go in for a closer inspection. He struggled to remember the details of what happened next; he had found his brother dead...

"Oh, look at this little guy!" came Desdaria's delighted squeal. Dezmond shot straight up, striking his head on something hard. The world shifted before his eyes as the moon set and the sun rose again, causing the shadows to dance around him.

Dezmond groaned. "Oh, sorry honey," Desdaria cooed as she kissed his smarting head. She was in her maternity gown, designed to show off her pregnancy. She was due any time and he, the expecting father, had been setting up some extra shelving in the nursery.

She passed the large toy in her hands to her husband. It was too large for the crib and its bottom half sagged, like a pet that didn't quite want to be carried but had grown accustomed to it. It was a combination of yellow and brown fur with tufts of white here and there, its trunk like that of an elephant but ending in a trumpet shape. The toy's glassy eyes stared up at him. "Anteater?" Dezmond asked his wife.

"What's an anteater?" Desdaria asked.

He had forgotten that during his prolonged incarceration much of the wildlife he had grown up with had been rendered extinct. "Well..." he thought about how best to answer the question. "It has a snout like this." He tried to wiggle its nose at her. It didn't feel like the soft plush of a stuffed toy. It felt like there was more to this creature than a bag of stuffing: it was warm, and the tip of its nose was cold and moist. Dezmond glanced down at the anteater in his arms. The toy was careful to maintain its vacant stare with Desdaria. For a second, he thought he felt something brushing against his trousers, and his arms sprang out, lifting the toy away from his person to check. Nothing. He lifted the toy over his head, peering at its bottom, searching for the tail tucked between its legs.

"What is it, my love?" Desdaria watched her husband with a mixture of annoyance and amusement.

He put the anteater toy down in the corner of the nursery and stepped away from it, watching it. "I thought I felt a mouse." He smiled and changed the subject. "Where did you get it?"

"I found it in one of your boxes we had in the spare room," she said. "I thought it was something that you grew up with." She crouched down to be at eye level with the large stuffed toy. "I think he's cute anyway," she said after some thought and patted it on the head.

The toy still stared straight ahead. "What shall we name him?" Desdaria asked, smiling up at her husband, who helped her to her feet.

"Name a toy?" He chuckled. "Seems like something we should leave to our son, don't you think?" He winked.

"Or daughter," she countered. "Think of it like practice for naming our baby."

"Our baby will be named Damien." Dezmond did his best to smile. The certainty in his voice annoyed his wife.

"Damien," she tried the name. "It sounds so ominous. Why not Liam or Sean?"

"Why not Serge or Jack?" Dezmond retorted, much to Desdaria's irritation.

"I'm going to make some lunch," she said. "I saw some berries in the garden. I might make a pie. And if you behave yourself, I might even let you have a slice."

As his wife left the room, Dezmond saw the toy scratch itself with its hind leg and then return to its static position, suspecting that he had seen it move.

"I'll finish up here," he called after Desdaria as he closed the door, sealing himself in with the creature. Not the brightest move for a Hunter, but it might give Desdaria the chance to escape if things went wrong.

Dezmond approached the creature with caution. It maintained a blank stare. Its ears were all wrong for an anteater, he realized. This one had patchy elephant ears.

When he was a child, he had seen an actual anteater at a zoo. He and Alistair were so excited by its very existence that they drew hundreds of pictures of the creature. It reminded them of the creatures they had seen in their father's old journals.

Pictures from his childhood appeared on the walls. Alistair had drawn one anteater in particular over and over again, though its ears were like those of an elephant. He had spelled out the name Norbert on each one of his drawings using his waxy crayons.

"Norbert..." Dezmond read out loud, watching the letters dance and shift on the paper. His mind refused to grasp the concept of letters but could apparently glean a whole word.

"Here, put this one up!" Alistair handed Dezmond another drawing. The anteater on this one was purple and yellow with large pink ears. At its feet were many miniature versions of the creature in a field of fuchsia grass. As Dezmond gazed at the drawing, the nursery transformed back to his childhood bedroom.

The stuffed toy sat upright on his brother's bed, its empty stare unmoving.

Dezmond stuck the paper to the wall. "Here?" he asked, glancing down at Alistair, who nodded.

"Uh-huh!" Alistair dragged the toy off the bed. "What do you think Norbert?" He held up the toy to give it the opportunity to inspect the artwork. It stared at the drawings for some time.

"That's got to be the ugliest thing I've ever laid eyes on," Dezmond said.

"You're just jealous because Norbert likes me bestest!" Alistair gave the toy a squeeze of pure affection, and Norbert seemed happier somehow.

"He's not even real!" Dezmond chided, hoping to coax the toy into life by antagonizing his sibling.

"Ye-huh!" he shot back. "If you don't think he's real, why did ya ask if he could sleep in your bed tonight?"

Dezmond didn't remember fighting about some stupid toy. Had they bought the toy at the zoo? He was sure that it had appeared soon after their trip, but he couldn't place when or how. His memories were fleeting, as though they were being rewritten.

"Because...." He failed to come up with a valid reason.

Norbert growled a low warning right before the shrill shriek of a woman falling caused Dezmond to take off in a panic. "Desdaria," escaped Dezmond's lips, forgetting the strange creature and his brother.

He ran down a labyrinth of halls that twisted and turned, ignoring the transformation of his childhood home to his own, until he stood at the top of the stairs, staring down at his crying wife. "Oh Damien," she whimpered, "I told you to put away your toys." She sat on the stairs, nursing her sprained ankle.

Damien was four years old and hiding behind the banister at the base of the stair, surrounded by a mess of abandoned toys. His newborn brother and sister were crying for their mother, startled awake by her scream. Damien started to cry too, worried that he had hurt her and afraid of the consequences for disobedience. "I pick up," he said tearfully, plucking his toy train and letter blocks from the stairs. "I pick up!" He wiped the snot and tears from his face with his sleeve.

Heart in his throat, Dezmond swooped down on his wife, but Desdaria put a tender hand to his lips, silencing him before he could speak. Her deep brown eyes relayed a message of urgency: Damien was just a convenient scapegoat. Her husband picked her up and carried her upstairs. "Damien, come!" he barked.

Damien stifled his tears as best he could, following his parents to the nursery.

"I saw something," Desdaria whispered into her husband's ear, keeping her voice low enough to avoid frightening her child. "You said that it was safe here." He could hear the fear in her tone. She had heard, through local gossip, the survivor stories of townships wiped out in recent demonic attacks, and she worried for the safety of her family. Their home was sitting close to the ever-shrinking safety zone's perimeter. She had been begging him to move closer to the capital, having already lost her father and one sister to demon raids.

"Are you sure?" he whispered back, terror striking at his heart. His children were defenceless and easy prey, yet he was bound by his family's heritage to teach them things children should never have to worry about. His family had been fighting against the demon uprising since before the rise of the Sumerian civilization. Even now, against these insurmountable odds, his bloodline was expected to maintain the duties as sworn by their cursed ancestor.

He didn't want to tell his wife that the demons would seek them out, even if they moved closer to the capital, just as they would seek the demons. It was this cursed mutual attraction that made his lineage so good at what they did.

"It moved fast like a shadow," she told him, "skittered across the stairs." Dezmond had shared only a few details of the Demon War with his young wife, just enough so she would recognize the signs of a demonic presence and get their family to safety.

He had to ask, "Are you sure it wasn't a mouse?"

She pinched him hard, causing him to stop to bear the pain or risk dropping her. It wasn't a mouse. She knew how a mouse moved, having grown up on a farm that often sheltered the pests. "It jumped at me and hissed. Its teeth... they weren't right, not like proper animal teeth."

He wanted to tell her she was imagining things, but knew that it wouldn't put her mind at rest. Desdaria could be so stubborn.

"Do you hear that?" Desdaria asked. She slipped out of Dezmond's arms and limped toward the nursery. It's strange how loud silence can be. Even Damien, who was lingering behind them, had stopped sobbing to listen for his newborn brother and sister.

Dezmond's heart leaped to his throat. Was that thing in the nursery?

He dashed down the hall toward the door marked with a small, sky-blue cloud sign that read, "Baby". With every step he took, the door slipped further away. Much to his frustration and relief, his wife pushed past him as she dashed down the growing hall. She seized the door handle and pushed the door open, leaving Dezmond far behind.

A brilliant light escaped the room when his wife entered it, washing out the world around him. For a moment, there was nothing but him, the sound of his heavy breathing, and his feet pounding against the hardwood floor – the boards twisted and warped, their brilliant colour fading to an ashy grime.

The door closed with a solid thud, denying the old man access to the nursery beyond. Desdaria's sobbing could be heard from inside. Dezmond pounded on the door in frustration, attempting to force the handle to give way. His wife stifled another sob, holding her breath as though hoping that with her silence, he'd go away.

He felt it before he saw it, and spun around as though facing the evil would somehow prevent its attack. The hall before him was consumed by darkness. He couldn't see the staircase that led to the main floor. Instead, it was just a hall, empty except for the living darkness that shifted into something nightmarish.

Hundreds of small red eyes gleamed into existence. Every one of them fixated on the frightened old man.

He couldn't think. He couldn't call up the archives of his memory to figure out what had hunted him down. All he knew was that this was not a mouse.

"Desdaria, open the door!" he shouted, pounding on its blistered surface. The monster growled, its breath reeking of sulphur, and the sound shook Dezmond as though the earth had opened up before him.

There was a scratching noise by his feet, like some puppy wanting to be let in. He risked a look down to see the anteater with the elephant ears scratching at the door. It whimpered a little and waited.

Its ears perked up when the lock turned on the other side. It looked up at Dezmond. The old man pushed on the handle, and the door swung open. Taking the anteater by the waist, he darted into the room and slammed the door shut behind him.

He and the strange creature listened for any sounds that suggested that the monster would give chase. After a moment, Dezmond slid to the ground with his back against the door and released the anteater from his arms.

It scratched itself before waddling away. Dezmond took in his surreal surroundings. The room that he found himself in was not a part of any home he'd ever lived in. It was unlike any place he had seen before, and yet it comprised the pieces of his life.

Towers of junk, reaching far into the sky above, cluttered the room. There were walls, crooked and painted in bright colours of the kind seen in modern paintings, but there was no roof. At the far end of the room, Alistair sat at a desk, facing a tall window that stretched above the walls by five feet. Despite there being no ceiling, the beam of moonlight shone only through this window.

After a moment, Dezmond stood and followed the path that the anteater had taken through the pillars of memories toward the only other person in the room. The anteater tugged on the child's pajamas, asking to be let up.

Alistair stopped writing to look down at his companion. "Did you find him?" he asked the anteater.

Excited, the creature spun at its master's feet and dashed toward the approaching Dezmond, as though to show the boy whom it had brought.

At the sight of him, the child launched from his seat and flung himself toward the old man, wrapping his arms around him in a tight hug. "Dez!" Tears fell from the boy's haunted eyes. Remembering himself, the boy pulled away.

The room felt too real. Thinking back to everything that had just happened, on how he'd got this far, the memories were fading fast, almost as though...

"Am I dreaming?" Dezmond asked no one in particular.

"Sort of. I guess the easy answer is yes, you are dreaming," Alistair replied. "We've been waiting for you, Norbert and I." The anteater with the elephant ears spun next to the child, happy with himself.

"What is this place?" Dezmond asked, taking a cautious step toward his sibling's workstation.

"This is a place between the real world and the dream world," Alistair said, returning to his journal. "When you go back to your dream, there's a good chance that you'll forget you were ever here." He kept his face hidden from Dezmond's view, but he could not hide the sadness in his voice. "I wanted to see you. I wasn't strong enough back then to tell you I was okay." The boy inspected the way the moonlight hit the surface of his shoes.

"But I'm stupid!" he cried, unable to hold back his tears. "Because of me the Nightmare got loose, and now you're stuck in a dream that you might never wake up from!" He fell in a heap on the floor, wiping tears from his face with his sleeve. "I just wanted to see you so bad!"

Dezmond crouched down by Alistair's side and placed a hand on his brother's head. "You must be lonely here," he said.

The boy sniffled. "No, not really. I have Norbert and the others. They've been very good to me. We're like a big family." He stared down at the floor a while longer. "Dez," he tried after a moment of silence. "Could you—I mean, would you stay here with me?"

Dezmond knew the answer immediately, but took his time to give Alistair the impression that he had at least considered it.

"I mean, you don't have anyone left. Your kids are all grown up and can take care of themselves. You could live in the dream world with me and I can teach you all sorts of things about the Dream Eaters!" Alistair looked up at his brother with big, hopeful eyes.

Dezmond wasn't sure if any of this was real. He was even less sure of the consequences of accepting the proposal. Despite himself, tempting possibilities played out in his mind. He could leave it all behind. He could create his own dream world to live in for the rest of eternity and never feel pain or suffering again. He could be its master, no longer subject to his oppressive destiny. It would be his last "Screw you!" to the gods.

The idea brought a smile to his face.

Norbert's long nose wrapped around his leg as the creature rested its head on the old man's lap, looking at him with its deep, soulful eyes, as though trying to communicate something. Dezmond scratched behind its ear.

"What happened that night? How did you get here?" he asked his brother, buying time.

"I was growing my moon berries. Back then, I didn't know that they were food for the Dream Eaters. In our world, they appear under a full moon, and a sick Dream Eater will eat the dream fruit to purify itself before coming back home. That night I saw the fruit, and I ate the berries. They were so pretty!" Alistair said.

He shot to his feet and pointed to the terracotta pot with a moon sigil inscription on the front, that was sitting on the desk in the moonlight. A strong, healthy plant had grown in the pot. It had indigo leaves with lilac veins. It was pretty in its oddness. Amongst its leaves, luminescent berries the size and colour of pearls waited to be plucked.

"These here aren't ready yet," Alistair said, pointing to them. "I ate these, but I know better now. If the Nightmare hadn't gotten to me, I would have been very sick, but I would have gotten over it. These here," he said as he pulled at two translucent berries, "these are the ones that can cure a sick Dream Eater."

He gave the berries to the excited Norbert, who grabbed them.

"I don't understand," Dezmond pondered out loud. "How was the Nightmare able to get to you?"

"The same way it got to you," Alistair replied. "Sometimes there are cracks between the dream world and the real one. The Nightmares sneak through. I don't think they know that they've crossed over. They just think it's still the dream world. But it's not."

He paused to pet Norbert. "In the dream world, the nightmare will go away as the Dream Eaters eat away at it. But in the real world..." Alistair hesitated. "In the real world, a Nightmare can make whatever you're afraid of real. It'll feed off your fear."

"You remember the thing mom used to say, that if you dreamed that you died in your sleep, you'd die in real life?" the boy said.

Dezmond nodded. "But that's nonsense."

"It used to be true when there wasn't a veil. I guess the idea just sort of stuck. Anyway, if a Nightmare has tracked you down in the real world, then it'll try to kill you. I don't think it means to," he added, looking down at his contented companion as he stroked the creature between the ears. "They get a taste for fear and don't know when to stop. They're just animals doing what comes naturally."

"You're saying that a Nightmare is just a sick Dream Eater?" the old man asked, trying to understand the concepts of the Dream Eaters and Nightmares.

Alistair nodded. "A Dream Eater eats dreams, including nightmares. If they eat too many nightmares, they start manifesting nightmares until they can be purified. Dream Eaters are the reason you can't remember your dreams when you wake up. Well... sometimes you can, but unless you hold onto them, they fade fast. That's because the Dream Eater is busy eating it."

Dezmond wondered why such a strange creature would exist. He couldn't imagine how it would go about eating a person's dreams. "It's a very important job," Alistair offered. "If a dream doesn't get eaten; it can become real."

It wasn't hard for the old man to understand why this would be an undesirable scenario. He had a reoccurring nightmare where he had to stay after school. In the stillness of the yawning darkness, vile fluid humanoid creatures danced in the halls. When the monsters inevitably spotted him, they'd give chase. He'd wake before the monsters tore him to pieces in their ravenous frenzy.

He couldn't leave that thing to wander out in the real world to target a new victim. "How do I stop the Nightmare?"

"I can't help you with that," Alistair said, bearing the look of a guilty conscience. "I'm stuck here forever, Dez."

"I asked how to stop it, not if you could come with me," Dezmond snapped in a tone harsher than he intended.

Shocked by his brother's response, Alistair fought back tears. He realized that the old man would not stay in the dream world with him. "You'll need to call it out," he said. "Do you know anything about lucid dreaming?"

"I do," Dezmond said. "It's a state where the dreamer has control over the dream."

"It's also the place where the dream world is the most real to the dreamer. If you get hurt while lucid dreaming, it'll happen to you in the real world too. You understand?" Alistair asked.

Dezmond nodded. "What do I need to do once I'm there?"

"Call up your darkest memory, re-create your living nightmare. The Nightmare will want to come out to feed." Alistair plucked a few berries from the plant and handed them to his brother. "Try feeding these to the Nightmare while you're in the dream world. That should be enough to get it to let you wake up. In the real world, you'll have to grow your own berries, the Dream Fruit. Catch the Dream Eater and feed it the berries in the real world too. Eventually it'll find its way back to its herd."

Norbert pulled at Dezmond and whined for the berries. The old man hoped that the Nightmare would feel the same way. He didn't like the idea of reliving the worst day of his life. Already the memories were shaping themselves in his mind. He knew that once he left his brother's dream, it wouldn't be long before the terror of that tragic day would engulf him.

Looking back to the nursery door through which he came, Dezmond watched the door to his dream blister and warp.

Alistair continued. "It's not always easy to remember that you're dreaming, so you'll have to train yourself by using a phrase or an object as a trigger, something that will tell you you're dreaming."

"You don't have to do this," Alistair tried one last time.

"I can't let that thing roam free," Dezmond said, facing the door that led to his darkest memories. He muttered to himself, "This is only a dream.

This is only a dream. This is only a dream."

When he opened the door, thick black smoke poured through, engulfing him. He looked back to find that his brother and the strange room had disappeared, however he felt Norbert brush against his legs and waddle deeper into the nightmare. Dezmond wondered what business the creature would have in his dreams. Panic struck him. If the potency of Dezmond's worst memory was strong enough to attract a Nightmare, then it stood to reason that if Norbert were to devoured the nightmare that spawned from the memory, it could corrupt the little creature turning him into a Nightmare. Dezmond would have to fend off two corrupt Dream Eaters.

The old man chased after Norbert, hoping to urge him back to Alistair, forgetting the key phrase he was supposed to repeat to remember that it was all a dream.

Through the doorway, rafters collapsed and the roaring of angry flames consumed Dezmond's home. He made his way through the rooms, looking for his family.

"Desdaria!" he cried out and smashed open the door to their bedroom. He heard voices in the next room, but every time he forced his way through, he found the room empty.

He heard his wife cry out. "Note! Oh God, Note! Please hold on!"

"Mom!" came Damien's voice. He was an adult now; he had returned home from university over the winter holidays. Dezmond remembered that they were downstairs on the main floor, though try as he might, he couldn't find the stairs. It didn't matter how far he ran or which hall he turned down, their voices rang as clear as if he was standing in the room with them.

"What have you done?" Desdaria's voice quivered with fear, anger, and despair.

"I-I didn't mean to," Damien stuttered.

"Get away from her!" His mother shouted at him.

"We have to get outside!" Damien returned with the same ferocity.

"I'd rather die in here than be eaten by the demons you called to us."

"Please, Mom!" Damien begged. "I can protect you from the demons!"

"Get away!"

"I'm sorry, Mom, but I have no choice."

Desdaria screamed, followed by the sound of her body hitting the floor.

Tears ran from Dezmond's eyes, a combination of grief and the smoke burning them. "Desdaria!" he called, smashing his way through a door that looked like the manor's entrance.

He stopped at the main staircase, confused and disoriented. Damien was coming from the family room, with his teenage sister, Note, in his arms. "Dad!" He was just as surprised to see his father as Dezmond was to see his son. "Quick, Mom's in the other room!"

Dezmond ran into the family room. A creature had already begun the gruesome work of consuming his wife. It was humanoid, wiry and thin, with pale skin marred by patches of rotting flesh, and wearing a tattered dress from a bygone era. The demon's face was frozen in a permanent, silent scream, its eyes nothing more than holes in its head.

Its boney fingers held Desdaria down with unnatural strength, just in case its prey woke as it consumed her soul.

"Get away from her!" Dezmond bellowed at the creature, pushing it away with his mind. The demon was flung across the room, smashing the gallery windows.

Suddenly, the fire exploded with renewed energy, shattering the windows that remained, and throwing Dezmond from the room. His ears were ringing. Someone hovered over him, speaking to him. "I'm dreaming," Dezmond muttered. "This is a dream," he repeated. The phrase sparked his memory. The dream world became real somehow. He felt the stagnant air and breathed in the smoke caused by the fire. The heat of the flames burned his skin.

He stood up, feeling every ache and pain that his old body suffered. His clothes were singed and his hands were stained with ash. The demon who had been standing over him had melted away with the surreal nature of the dream.

The dream had merged with reality, and it would remain that way until he lost control over the lucid dream or defeated the Nightmare.

"ENOUGH OF THIS!" Dezmond roared.

The Nightmare leaped from the shadows, landing on all fours. It was the size of a lion with two rows of glowing red eyes along its skull and a tail that slithered with reptilian grace. The pointed tip on its long, thin nose was designed to impale the dreamer and suck out the dream. The corrupted Dream Eater had lost its charming elephant ears.

The Nightmare growled, stepping toward its prey, and the illusion of the dream world stuttered, taking Desdaria and his family with it. Dezmond realized, as he searched for the berries in his pockets, that the dream was an elaborate trap. He had been the Nightmare's prey all along.

Despite expecting the berries to be there, he found himself surprised when his fingers located them. They were harder than he expected, like handling pearls. He pulled them out, revealing them to the Nightmare.

The Nightmare paused, inspecting its prey and the offering. Its red eyes grew wide as its nose danced across the surface of Dezmond's hand, cool and wet, trailing blood across the old man's soiled palm.

To his surprise, the Nightmare began to dance like an excited puppy, spinning and whining. A dance that looked familiar.

Dezmond threw the first berry into the air and watched the Nightmare's nose snap up and plunge it into its monstrous maw as its face split into four pieces.

The creature's face returned to normal, and the dance resumed. Dezmond's felt his hold over the dream slip as his weight of his mind grew heavy and hazy, lulling him into a deeper state of the Dream World. He threw the last of the berries just as the dream consumed him.

☙❧

Dezmond lay face down on the hardwood floor. He felt a small tongue in his ear, urging him to wake, and paws pulling at his vest. He heard the worried half whine of an animal who wanted to help but was powerless to do so.

It cried out when it was pulled away, clinging to the fallen old man but forced to let go.

Dizzy and disoriented, Dezmond sat up. His suit was ruined, stained in his own blood. He searched for the wreckage of the manor's collapse but found none. His bodyguard, Philip, stood over him, holding the struggling Dream Eater to his chest.

Dezmond recognized the creature as Norbert. How is it he came to be here? Was he the infected Nightmare?

Norbert kicked at Philip's arms to free himself, when that didn't work, he opted for a different tactic: allowing his bottom half to sag, hoping to slip out of his captor's grasp, his toes searching for the ground that was still a foot away.

Norbert looked miserable in his defeat.

"You can put him down," Dezmond ordered Philip, who released his grip.

The Dream Eater slipped from the bodyguard's hold, bouncing toward Dezmond, who sat up to greet him. Norbert's small hands grabbed at Dezmond's fingers as his nose brushed against the old man's face before settling around his neck in a hug.

Philip regarded the scene, waiting for his next order. "This is Norbert," Dezmond introduced his aide to the creature while patting it on the head. "I imagine that he'll be with us for quite some time." He smiled at Norbert. "At least until I can return you to Alistair."

There was so much that Dezmond had to learn about the world, beyond the humans and demons that had plagued them for centuries. He hoped that some of the old family journals might hold the answers to help this creature make its way home. He would start with his father's, which he knew held the illustrations that he and his brother had been fond of.

❦ STORY II ❧
THE GAME: BETA TESTING

THE GAME: BETA TESTING

The Council Academy's auditorium buzzed with nervous energy and excitement as the students, dressed in costumes suited for their roles, rehearsed lines with dramatic flare.

Every December, like clockwork, the theatrical festivities aired live across the nation. The former government considered frivolous entertainment a waste of time, desiring instead for the population to focus their time and energy on intellectual and physical pursuits. As a reward, they had allowed for a small period at the end of the year for community entertainment. The current government, known as the Council, took a more measured approach. Though they shared much of the same attitude toward the overabundance of time-wasting activities, they acknowledged the need for the population to unwind and engage in social activities as a community, as long as the activities adhered to the strict government guidelines.

Each school presented several teams for the showcase, each team capable of winning valuable funding for their place of education. Knowing that government funding was won based on the number of parents watching their children on the live stream, it was not uncommon for struggling education centers to create a large cast of characters and force students into insignificant roles.

The Council's Academy didn't rely on viewership for government subsidies since the elite funded them through increasing tuition costs. The elite sent their children to the Academy for four things: education, opportunity, connections, and notoriety in one of three educational branches.

Contributions won from tonight's event would be donated, in whole, to charity. These public acts of charity improved the reputation of the school, the students taking part, and their parents, who would boast about their children's event rankings and scores. Everything at the Council's Academy was a competition. Everything that could be measured was judged and ranked.

Academy students measured their lives by those scores.

They coaxed and bullied high-ranking peers into participation if they thought it would improve their personal score, and competed for spotlight roles. The few students who were in a comfortable rank could opt instead to work behind the scenes.

As with every year, for the past three years, Seth was asked to star in the production. But there were only so many lead roles to go around, and he felt it best to leave the higher stress roles to those who needed to secure their rank. Unlike previous years, he was forced into it.

Seth had wound up getting punished while covering for a friend. It had been a gamble, but it was worth it. He could sacrifice the hour detention and slight hit to his reputation. The penalty against his friend, Astral, would have been more severe, and she could not afford to work for free for a solid month, plus handle an increased study workload, and maintain her Hunter's duties in secret.

But the teacher took pity on him because, as she said, "A good guy like you should know better than to stick his neck out for troublemakers.", and as a result, she assigned Seth to a lead role to undo the damage to his score.

To make matters worse, he later learned that his friend was innocent of the crime they had accused her of, and instead was a result of the actions of one William Mathers, whose pursuits for recognition often caused unnecessary friction.

Jealous that both Seth and Astral were invited to participate in active on-screen roles, he forced himself into a speaking role at the event, and somehow got onto the same production as Seth's sidekick. How the little narcissist landed an on screen role on such short notice was beyond him, but Seth wagered that William had sold his soul for the opportunity.

There were days that Seth felt like William was stalking him.

The dressing room was cramped with carts of handmade costumes, props, and shared dressing tables. Seth struggled to adjust his stage make-up as another student pushed his way in front of the mirror to adjust his hair, and pick at his teeth.

"Got all of your lines memorized, Mr. Hero?" William said, nudging Seth in the ribs. William was shorter than Seth by a foot and had wild brown hair, which he was growing out partly to spite his father, and partly because he felt his dishevelled appearance would give him that bad-boy look that girls found irresistible.

Seth had to commend William on his attention to such superficial details. He knew what it took to get what he wanted, even if it meant socially sabotaging his best friend. Seth felt like he was always guessing at people's motivations. He preferred to focus on doing the best that he could, and then he might have a bright future ahead of him.

Seth had dark, shoulder length hair, which was within acceptable parameters of the school code. His build was athletic, as in recent years he had begun building muscles over his otherwise wiry frame. Seth nodded, taking the opportunity to adjust his costume as the peering actor who had taken up the mirror opted to chase after a stage hand with personal directives that would no doubt improve the play.

"Nicole must have wanted to practice that kissing scene with you like a million times. You think Astral was jealous?" William grinned.

"How could she be? She didn't turn up to any of the practices." Seth thought Astral was a little more responsible than that. He had taken the time to practice his lines and dedicate them to memory, paying careful attention to the direction offered by his team leader. Astral, on the other hand, couldn't even fake an interest, often expressing that the whole event was a waste of time.

"I heard she's with a different group," William whispered as though it was a clandestine conspiracy theory.

"Who's with a different group?" Nicole asked as she entered the boys side of the dressing room. Her smile was wide and toothy. Seth knew that she meant to be friendly, but he found the exposure of her teeth unsettling. The way her lips moved, as though trying to avoid contact with each other, made him think she had applied something to her teeth.

"Earth to Seth," she sang, trying her best not to look offended.

"Sorry, go ahead," he said. She was a faux blonde, but took enough care to hide her dark roots. Her hair had been styled in a late 1920s look and set into an immovable mass, a picture of perfection, and all wrong for the medieval time period in which the student play was set.

"A bunch of us are planning to get together tonight for a little after-party. We'd like it if you'd come," she said.

If it was going to be anything like her "one last late-night practice session", Seth could do without it. But behind her, he could see William trying to get his attention. His excitement at the opportunity to wine and dine with the social committee and some of their elite friends was almost palpable – he didn't seem to understand that the invitation was meant only for Seth.

Seth smiled and nodded, he hated large gatherings but he'd show up with William, set him loose, and then disappear while the young student made a spectacle of himself.

"I'd like to bring a guest, if that's okay?"

William's face lit up in thanks. Seth hoped that the term "guest" was vague enough that Nicole would make other assumptions. He watched the flashes of emotion playing across her over-powdered face: irritation, indignation, and finally acceptance as she devised a workaround to her false assumptions. She hadn't even noticed William, so Seth assumed that she thought he intended to bring Astral, who he was rarely seen without.

He had heard elites refer to Astral as "Seth's charity project". Sometimes that was true. These days he felt like he was circling her to keep the hungry sharks at bay, but Astral didn't indicate that she cared about, or even noticed, the other students.

"Great!" Nicole tried to sound excited. She moved in closer to him, her body only a few inches from his own. She added in a seductive tone, "I'll see you later," then tried to move in for a quick kiss.

He turned his head, causing her to plant her kiss on his cheek. She often liked to linger with her unwanted kisses, as though he'd become enamoured with her if she sucked the soul from his body.

Her hips swayed invitingly as she exited the dressing area. She cast one last glance over her shoulder and winked before vanishing into the chaos of the dressing room.

"She so wants you," William said.

"She's not exactly subtle, is she?" Seth sighed.

"What's your problem? She's so hot. If I were in your shoes I would—"

"You'd finish before you even got started," Seth cut in.

The lights dimmed, signalling five minutes until showtime. Which was fortunate, because this was not a conversation he wanted to carry on with William, of all people. He reminded Seth of a horny Chihuahua, dick hanging out and begging for a little touch. He found it revolting.

Seth pulled on his long, dark blue velvet jacket. It cut off at the ankle, accentuating his height – now past the six-foot mark, but did little for practical combat. His shirt hung open, revealing his bare chest, over pants that were a little too tight and made it difficult to walk without an odd gait. Overall, he felt that this combination of apparel was more of a fan service, rather than playing to any historical accuracy.

Much of the cast wore outrageous fantasy costumes. For a moment, Seth pictured Astral happily pretending to be a sheep somewhere. It seemed to be the consensus among his peers that an Enhanced student shouldn't even be in the production and therefore deserved as little screen time as possible. Since her status as an Enhanced remained undetermined in the court of public opinion, they couldn't outright ban her from the production, at the behest of the faculty. After more thought, he figured she'd try to get the sheep to revolt against their shepherds in a humiliating but just spectacle. She'd go off script, just to see how long it would take for the entertainment committee to pull her from the live stream.

Translucent spheres, referred to as personal digital pods, filled the auditorium. The pods were big enough to hold a full-grown human being, and each projected a pre-programmed setting for every character to act within, independently of the action taking place in another. The computer would dictate the camera angles based on the script, similar to a professional broadcast production, though there was always a human element lingering behind the scenes, ready to take control in case the algorithm failed.

Seth assumed his position within the auditorium.

The world around him vanished as a brilliant white light surrounded him. A booming voice filled his pod. "In a land far, far away, where magic is real and princesses need saving..."

The script was terrible, making use of every cliché imaginable. He knew that he was playing out some deranged fantasy that was the culmination of every "cool" thing the writing group had ever seen, without factoring in things like context. He had heard that the production had been dreamed up and written in two days. To Seth, this was a bad sign. To everyone else, it was an indication of pure, unquestionable genius, worthy of awe.

The story had warring nations, forbidden love, a rogue prince, two love triangles, and poorly timed slapstick comedy scenes and one-liners. He hoped that other teams had fared better with their classical productions, though he had heard that there were plans to sync all teams into one overlapping story arc. It seemed ambitious for students who didn't know the limits of their creative talents.

The world around him began to take shape. He stood at the foot of a dark, foreboding castle. Lightning streaked across the sky, revealing the silhouettes of several crumbling towers. In one of those, his princess was awaiting rescue. If this hero had any sense, he'd go back home.

Seth gazed up at the castle before him a little longer. As the hero of the story, he was to fight his way through throngs of minions, each more powerful and cleverer than the last, and when he reached the top, he would engage in a climactic duel of magic versus steel, where steel would vanquish all. Or was it love? It was supposed to be love.

He had to push Nicole from his mind or else risk insubordination. He figured that the hero could live a quiet life in the country and let everyone think the dragon had eaten him. Who needs fame and glory? But without a hero, there wouldn't be a story to tell.

There would be a dragon. There was always a dragon.

He looked around for some sheep on the verge of rebellion, then sighed as he held out his hand and visualized a sword. In response, the digital world provided a long, slim blade, complete with decorative engravings, which formed in his hand. He would go through the catacombs because the direct approach would have been too easy and not as entertaining.

He had rehearsed each scene in isolation as part of the director's plan to keep reactions genuine. They kept the scene with the dragon top secret, though he rehearsed a mock battle. Rumour had it they were testing a digital platform to assist in training, and this dragon was a part of that program.

If it weren't for the general lack of smells, Seth could have immersed himself fully in this digital world. He trudged through the flooded catacombs, his boots making a wet sucking sound as they pried themselves from the ground. It didn't seem likely that he would be able to sneak up on the horde lurking beyond the thick webs of the neglected subterranean passage.

It wasn't long before he reached his first mark.

He remained in the shadows, watching his skeletal peers recite their poor lines as best they could without laughing at themselves. It was easy to forget that they were being watched by millions.

"... I mean, really, who goes around reviving skeletons? We've got to be the most inefficient fighters," one skeleton said. It was a commentary that Seth had heard a few times before, but he couldn't quite recall where from.

"Seriously, look!" the skeleton pulled off a boney arm and slapped his companions one by one like a row of keys on a piano. "It just came right off! If we go charging at this hero jerk, how are we supposed to know that we'll still have all of our limbs by the time we reach him!"

"I suppose there's only one way to find out." Seth stepped into the light and fell forward, his boots lodged in the thick, ankle-deep sludge. Wet and muddied, he glared up at the skeletons, who burst out laughing.

If his castmates had been demons, he'd be dead. Seth felt himself flush. He had damaged his reputation as a skilled fighter with just a few bumbling actions.

He pulled himself to his feet, but as he tried to move, he fell forward once again, the mud holding its grip on him. The skeletons exchanged confused looks before approaching the hero. "What's going on, man?" A boney hand wrapped around his leather boots and gave his leg a tug. "He's stuck!"

"This isn't supposed to happen," another commented. Seth glared at him. The last thing the director told his actors at rehearsal was "when in doubt, remain in character". Seth took this to mean that they should never acknowledge that something had gone off script. He unfastened his boots and pulled his legs free, but he still couldn't wrench his footwear from the mud. They were frozen in position. There was no give, no sense of suction.

The digital environment didn't feel right, as though faulty code was creating odd glitches. The catacombs flickered as thunder rolled overhead. "I think your boots are gone," one skeleton said, pointing to the shoes as they disappeared beneath the muddy surface. "Seriously, I didn't think mud did that."

With sludge squeezing between his toes, Seth sloshed his way toward the skeletal group. He sank a little with each step and was suddenly afraid of what would happen if someone hadn't thought to program a bottom to the catacomb passage.

The skeletons grabbed onto his arms and lifted him from the mud, buying him a few more precious moments. "I think we'll need to escort Mr. Hero," one skeleton said to the others, who nodded in agreement.

Though it was off script, Seth was grateful for the help. He'd never make it to his next scene with the production working against him. "Don't worry, we can have our big fight scene on solid ground ahead," another skeleton volunteered.

The muddied water gurgled and bubbled behind them. Rising from the mud, a new horde of skeletons emerged. "Who are these guys? Hey,

BUDDY! We got this!" His skeletal support remained oblivious to the threat. Unless the costume designers had improved their talents since the start of the production, these creations were not actors. Seth wondered if the code was built using remnants of a different program.

Pieces of rotting flesh hung from their bones, barely stringing together the anatomy needed for cohesive functionality. Dislocated jaws, teeth missing, many of them had lost the odd arm. They clung to rusted, menacing weapons: axes, swords, maces.

"Launch me," Seth told his skeletal companions. "Throw me hard and far." The program wanted to claim him for some nefarious purpose. It didn't seem to matter if it claimed him dead or alive, but the least he could do was ensure that no one else got caught in its trap. He would sort out the details later. If he survived.

"You'll never be able to take them on your own," one of the cast of skeletons argued.

"Do you want to fight them?" he inquired. They wouldn't have to. They were instructed to phase out of the production as soon as Seth was off screen, assuming the program would let them. He decided not to think about that little detail. As sinister as the situation had become, he didn't want to spend the rest of his life in the same digital space as Nicole.

"On three!" The skeletal crew lifted Seth and swung him back and forth.

"ONE!"

"TWO!"

The rotting skeletons charged. Empty eye sockets could not see what lay ahead, but the booming voices of Seth's castmates gave them a direction to attack.

"THREE!" They launched Seth toward the undead.

As he soared through the air, he knew instantly that he hadn't gained enough height to go over the menacing horde. Instead, he bowled them over, their weapons scraping his skin and tearing at his costume. He bit back against the pain, focusing on getting to his feet and taking off at a run. "Get out of here!" Seth shouted to the cast of skeletons, unsure if they realized the danger that they were in. It was a small relief to glimpse them pop out of the digital space.

Seth reached for the sword at his hip, then cursed when he found nothing. Having lost his weapon in his initial fall, he had no way to fight against the undead horde chasing him. He held out his hand and visualized a weapon. Nothing. The digital space wasn't responding to the commands the production crew had taught him.

The mud felt like millions of tiny hands pulling at him, desperate to hold on as he tried to run away. His next mark was up ahead, but shouldn't have been so far. There were no turns or added passages, just one narrow path to follow. The pursuing skeletons splashed some distance behind him.

He was waist deep in the muddied catacombs by the time he reached the stone steps that led to the next segment of this disastrous play. He pulled himself up the first few steps and crawled until he was free of the mud's persistent pull. In the darkness, he couldn't make out much beyond the tricks of his mind. He thought for a gruesome moment that the mud was comprised of thousands of gripping tendrils, withering back into the recesses of the catacomb passage.

Each deep breath he took burned a little less. He listened, closing his eyes and straining his senses. He heard nothing. But he knew that the skeletons were still searching for him in the darkness.

He might have time to warn William before they reached them.

Seth ascended the uneven, worn stone stairs to the next part of the play. Torches lit the intersecting corridors, revealing the dusty remnants of ancient decor. Ahead were the remains of an old statue standing in front of a frayed, two-coloured tapestry, which was now black with fungus. The statue held a heroic pose, with an armored boot stomping the skull of a dragon. Head held high, the hero jutted his muscular chest to the gods, sword pointed to the sky. The sword was missing, and most of the statue's arms were broken off. The element of foreshadowing made Seth nauseous.

Fighting a dragon in this environment would be suicide.

At this intersection, he was supposed to meet the bumbling thief, as played by William. The boy was nowhere to be found. "William!" Seth hissed into the darkness. Despite his feelings for William, he hoped that he hadn't run into similar problems.

William was meant to steal the jeweled sword from the ancient statue ahead of him. The statue would come to life and attack them. Thinking it wiser to travel as a team, the thief would join the hero and even offer to share a paltry portion of his loot.

With no arms, there was no sword.

Seth heard the light steps of the undead echoing from the stairwell. He plucked a torch from the wall to gauge the distance, finding that the number of stairs he had climbed had lessened. The black, muddied waters of the catacombs reflected the torch light. He swallowed his fear. He had less time than he thought.

He turned back and inspected the heroic figure. The remains of the arms were shattered at the base. Judging by rubble that littered the ground, the hand and sword were missing. This wasn't the work of a malicious program gone rogue. Someone had tampered with the exit of the scene, knowing that the statue would come to life.

Seth crouched to get a better look at the base, noting heavy scores in the stone on which it sat. He ran his fingers through the dust, leaving a clean trail in their wake. William had activated the hidden passage behind the statue. Did that thief think he could steal the show? Seth wouldn't have put it past him.

His script knowledge told him he needed the sword to lodge in the keyhole hidden behind the tapestry, and he'd need the strength of two to move the statue by force. How had William managed the feat on his own…

Seth pushed the tapestry aside. A broken sword was lodged in the socket, half turned, and the narrow passage lay open, just wide enough to let someone with William's build squeeze through. He had only activated enough of the sequence to get the job done. In typical William style, everything was done in half-measures. Not well, just good enough, while leaving everyone else to deal with the mess he left behind.

The space wasn't wide enough for Seth to push through. He feared that the passage would close on him should he try. "Well, if William can half-ass his way out…" Seth returned the torch to its bracket and pulled up his sleeves.

He strained against the heavy statue, pushing it a few more inches away from the exit. He cringed at the loudness of the stone giving way.

A heavy axe lodged itself into the statue's front, the skeletal horde having mistaken the heroic figure for Seth. The hero's head fell from its marble shoulders, breaking to pieces as it hit the ground and spurring the skeletons into a frenzy over the remains. Seth couldn't continue to move the statue into position, not without getting caught in the onslaught.

He glanced at the passage, was it wide enough? He stepped back from the ravaging horde and slipped behind the tapestry, praying that he hadn't made a sound. But he couldn't squeeze into the tight passage. He had no choice. He had to fight.

He pulled on the tapestry, tearing it free, and blanketed the skeletal horde. Like the unthinking, savage creatures they were, they lashed out, catching one another in the confusion. Seth launched at them, praying they were more brittle than they appeared and hoping he wouldn't accidentally impale himself on their weapons.

He aimed low, dodging the swing of a mighty sword and forcing his fist through a brittle torso. With a firm hold on the skeleton's spine, he pulled it through its ribcage as the creature flailed, tearing holes in the tapestry. Seth spun, kicking high, separating torso from legs and propelling them into its comrades. The legs and torso operated as two separate entities, thrashing about for a fresh kill.

An almighty axe protruded from the tapestry, caught in a skeletal grip, preparing to swing. Seth reefed the weapon free from the skeleton. The heavy, two-handed weapon wasn't ideal to manage, but Seth found that if he balanced it just right and made good use of the momentum, he could keep the weapon from weighing him down.

He danced through the confused horde, using each glancing blow against his foes to fuel the momentum he needed to move and take another swing at his assailants. In a few minutes, Seth reduced the skeletons to a pile of broken bones. He brought the weapon down, crushing the remaining skull, before pausing to adjust his bloodied shirt.

Moving onward, Seth pushed the hacked remains of the statue until it wouldn't go any further, and the passage behind opened wide with a loud rumbling, calling new monstrosities to his location. Though easier to move now, he noted that the base of the statue pushed back against his grip, wanting to return to its resting position. He slammed the axe down behind the statue, lodging it into place before he dashed down the passage to the courtyard.

Rain beat down on him. It was neither warm nor cold, just wet. The storm had gained momentum, a theatrical reference to the danger that awaited him. Across the courtyard, the doors to the main hall were open. Someone had gone in ahead of him.

Seth raced toward the hall while trying to keep under cover, ducking down behind shrubs and looking for signs of more monsters. When he reached the entrance, he peered inside, spotting William wandering around and muttering to himself. "William!" Seth said, just loud enough to catch the boy's attention. The boy jumped as though caught stealing a snack before dinner.

"Seth, I'm so glad to see you," he said as Seth stepped into the hall. Seth closed the door and bolted it behind him just in case another mob of undead made an appearance. "You wouldn't believe the nightmare I've been through," William continued.

"Does it have anything to do with leaving me stranded in the catacombs?" Seth growled.

"Oh, um..." William searched for a valid reason to have left his companion in the lurch. "I had no choice. It was move on or..."

"I understand," Seth said. He wondered whether he would have done the same in William's situation if his options were to push forward or be killed, and he felt guilty for thinking the worst of him.

"I knew you'd get it," William said. Something in his tone made Seth suspicious. It could have been the way he looked past Seth for the next objective, or the way he still held the broken half of the gilded key blade in his grip. Would William turn on him if it meant his chance to shine as the hero?

Somewhere close by, a howl called out. Seth brushed it off as added atmosphere until he heard clawed paws tapping against the stone floor. Three heads and three pairs of glowing red eyes appeared in the darkness. The hell hound drooled at its prey.

He cursed himself for not having the forethought to grab one of the ruined weapons. "Give me your sword," Seth ordered William. He kept his voice low and his eyes on the beast. He wasn't sure if he was supposed to make eye contact with a dog to assert his authority, or if he was better off lowering his eyes and playing a submissive role. His focus moved from one head to the next, unsure if he had made the right decision. Astral was so much better at these things.

"No way! Where's your sword?" William countered, pulling his half sword to his chest.

Seth cringed at William's loudness, but he realized that the dog was watching him and not his companion. "I had to leave it behind. I couldn't summon another one," Seth said, trying to keep his voice even and nonthreatening so as not to spur the hound into an attack. He changed tactics. "Fine, you fight the dog. I'll go find the dragon."

"What? You can't leave me here all by myself!" William shouted. The dog charged, each head barking with the promise to bite.

The pair ran. It wasn't long before William vanished from sight, having slipped through a door and bolted it shut behind him. Seth banged on the door, demanding to be let in.

The dog's deep growls caused him to spin around, pressing his back to the door.

"Seth, you okay out there?" William asked.

"Bloody fantastic. You?" Seth said.

"No need to get snippy."

The dog jumped for Seth's throat. He rolled out of the way, causing the massive hound to throw itself against the door, which cracked with the impact. Furious barks and growls drowned out William's screams. The heads couldn't seem to agree on a target.

Seth took his opportunity to run. With the game of chase in progress, the hell hound opted to leave the thief behind in favour of the hero. The dog remained close on his heels, nipping at him when it had the opportunity. Seth veered off, taking sharp turns and keeping his movements as unpredictable as he could, causing the dog to slide a little too far down a corridor and lose precious seconds.

One wrong turn and he realized that he had made a serious mistake. His path ended with a set of large, engraved double doors. He prayed that they were unlocked.

Reaching them, he fumbled with the door handles, his sweaty palms not gripping the way they should. Finally, the door opened and he slid inside, closing it behind him and pressing his back against it. The hell hound bashed itself against the ornate wood.

"Here, use this." In the dark he couldn't see what was being handed to him, but it felt long and heavy, and it was just the right size for his hand to fit into the looped handles. The dog pounded against the door, testing its strength. It would hold.

"Thank you," he told the voice that he sensed was somewhere to his left. He thought back to the script to place who he was meant to encounter at this stage.

"You're very welcome." He knew that voice. In the dark, he heard the clear ring of youthful innocence with a mix of playfulness.

"Astral?"

"Yes, Seth," she replied.

"I thought they would have given you a simple role like a sheep," he told her.

"No. Not a sheep," she said, irritated.

He hoped that he hadn't offended her.

He couldn't quite place the scene in his memory. "Am I in the wrong area?" he asked her.

"You're here for the dragon?"

"Yes. I mean, I guess so."

She was silent.

"Astral?" He couldn't sense her presence near him. He felt around; she had to be nearby.

"It went that way." In the dark, he couldn't see which way she was pointing, but the sound of her voice gave him some point of reference. He tried to reach for her hand to figure out which way was "that way". He could've sworn she was doing this on purpose, as though she didn't want him to find what he was looking for.

Seth froze. "Do you hear that?" he asked.

"The dog?" The hell hound had resorted to scratching and sniffing at the door while whining. The dog was a lot less threatening when it sounded like a lost puppy.

"No, not that," he replied.

They listened. He narrowed his eyes as a thought occurred to him. "Take a step that way." In the dark, she couldn't see which direction he was pointing in either, so she opted to take a step back.

Squeak!

It had a rubbery sound to it, short and to the point.

Squeak!

"Oh, that's me!" she exclaimed.

Squeak! Squeak! Squeak!

"Why are you making that sound?"

He heard her shuffling. In a moment, he felt something press against his body. It was large enough to require both hands to hold, yet it was very light and had a texture like felt. At its tips, it had smooth, hard rubber claws attached to it. It might have been footwear. He squeezed it.

Squeeeeeeeeak.

"Are you the dragon?" he asked Astral. That was unsurprising. His friendship with this strange girl had caused divisions among his peers. Having him kill her was a symbolic act for those students who felt that he could do better than be friends with someone who bore the traits of an Enhanced.

"No, I don't think so. I'm a dinosaur!" she offered. Her innocence rang aloud, she truly believed that she was a dinosaur.

He felt for her hands but found none. He felt for her face. She must have assumed that he was looking for her because she pushed her costume in his general direction. Much like her footwear, her head was made of felt. There were two big, glass eyes on either side, a hard horn on the tip of her nose and two more on the top of her head. She was the dragon, and they had set out to make her look ridiculous. His heart sank.

"What makes you think you're a dinosaur?" he said to her.

"I don't have wings," then added as an afterthought, "or breathe fire."

"Sound logic, with the exception that dinosaurs don't speak."

"How do you know? When was the last time you met a dinosaur?" The tone in her voice told him that there would be no reasoning with her.

A moment of silence passed between them.

There was a rap at the door. "Seth?" came William's voice. "Let me in."

He was tempted to leave the thief at the mercy of the hell hound, but that wouldn't be very hero-like.

Seth removed the mysterious, two-handled object from against the door. In the light, he saw William's wide, boyish grin, oblivious that he had done anything wrong at all. "You just hanging out in the dark?" he asked as he stepped inside.

Seth closed the door once again and barricaded it in case the hound returned.

"Oh yeah, did you find the dragon? Oh, wait. Let me get the lights."

It was quiet for a moment as William searched for something in his pockets. "Illuminate," he stated, and the orb he was holding lit up and hovered in front of them.

Seth saw William turn two shades paler right before he said "Extinguish" in a high-pitched voice.

"Seth, there's a dragon right next to you," William said.

Seth grabbed the orb from William and issued the command. "Illuminate." He turned to Astral. "I know—"

Tink! went the orb as it hit the ground then rolled toward the dragon.

Small as the orb was, it had enough power to light up half of the room, while casting the rest in obscure and terrifying shadows. It also revealed Astral's costume in its full glory. Her head alone was the size of Seth's personal digital pod. The rest of her body could barely fit in the room. Ebony scales as thick as any armor he had seen covered her massive frame, and huge, glowing blue eyes stared down at him.

"You're not a dinosaur!" he gasped. He decided that she was much less intimidating in the dark. Her long tail swayed, accidentally knocking down pillars behind her reptilian form.

The dinosaur costume he had assumed was her stood in front of him, empty and shoeless. He saw that Astral had one shoe impaled on one of her claws and was working at trying to remove it, like crud stuck under her fingernail. Her impaled footwear squeaked in resistance.

William glanced from Seth to the dragon. "No shit that's not a dinosaur." He regarded his friend dubiously. "Why are you talking to it? You need to kill it!"

The dragon stared down at the thief. "Are you sure you want to do that?" she asked. Her voice was low and comforting, like a purr he felt vibrate throughout his body.

"Astral?" William drew his weapon. "Why would they make you the dragon?"

She curled up, folding her claws in front of her. "Someone has got to be the dragon," she replied. "I think I make a good dragon." She had known of her peers plan all along.

"You're a lame dragon," William hissed. He had no doubt about which crowd he was pandering to. William charged, weapon drawn, ready to dive into her ebony hide. She watched him like he was a bug stuck under a glass. His sword shattered against her scales.

"That hurt," she said.

William stumbled back, his sword useless. He hadn't been invited to do the fight scene with the dragon; therefore, he remained oblivious to how to bring about the dragon's bloody end.

"You're not playing fair," William whined. "You're supposed to die."

She blinked her big dragon eyes at him, then regarded Seth, who shrugged. "The script says I kill the dragon, fight the wizard, and save the princess."

Astral huffed a big sigh. "But what if I want to save the princess?"

"You wha—" He arched a brow. Nicole would just love that. He smiled. The play had veered so far off script that he didn't see a problem with the dragon saving the princess.

She continued, "Why do dragons always have to be the bad guys? I mean, I was just minding my business, and you came bursting in trying to kill me! I didn't even know there was a princess before now! I think I'm offended." She huffed again and rested her head in her claws. He noticed she was sitting right in front of the door.

"The princess will reward you with a kiss and her hand in marriage," Seth offered, hoping to dissuade her from saving the princess herself.

She considered this. "Doesn't she want her freedom? Will that not suffice? Is this some weird human mating ritual that I'm not aware of? Accuse some dragon of kidnapping her and wait for a hero to rush in to save the day and kill the poor unsuspecting dragon? I'm a victim here!"

"Can I go rescue the princess now?" William asked. "I mean… can Seth go rescue the princess now?"

Despite the sheer size of her eyes and the lack of irises and pupils, William knew that she was staring at him.

He poked her with the hilt of his broken sword, as if to antagonize her. Seth watched him for a moment. Eventually, she'd just breathe fire on William and that would be the end of him. Seth was sure that she could breathe fire. After all, he could see the wings she had claimed she didn't have. Granted, she didn't have the room to expand them.

"William, stop that," he ordered, then addressed the dragon. "They kidnapped you?"

"I don't know about kidnapped. I imagine so. There's a whole slave trade when it comes to big mythological creatures," she replied, sounding annoyed by the idea. "I'm not here of my free will, if that's what you're asking."

"It is," Seth said. "Am I right to assume that you are a lady?"

"I am of the female sex." She narrowed her giant eyes and growled, "Where are you going with this, hero?"

"You could classify yourself as a damsel in distress," he hinted.

She thought about it. "Sure, why not."

"You're not supposed to free the dragon, Seth!" William shouted as Seth pried the broken weapon from his resistant grip, which ended with the thief on his back on the cold stone floor.

Sword in hand, Seth proceeded to the back of the dragon where he found an enchanted manacle binding her to the floor. She wouldn't be able to move beyond this room if she tried.

Seth plunged the broken sword into the locking mechanism and twisted. The manacle popped open without a fuss.

William flushed with rage, but it was soon replaced with a mischievous smile. "Now you have to kiss Seth," he teased the dragon. "It's what the damsel does when she's rescued."

Astral's massive head spun to face Seth, who had backed up against a pillar to make room. "Is that true, Seth?"

He was too close to her nostrils, from which he was sure fire could spit out if he didn't word his answer right. "Yes, I-I suppose so," he said.

She considered this. A tongue whipped out from between intimidating teeth and ran up the length of his body to his face, lifting him a few feet off the ground. He was left feeling confused, flustered, and damp.

"No, not with your tongue!" William shouted. "People don't kiss other people by licking them."

"But I don't have any lips," Astral replied.

The hero shook himself. "Whatever." He cut William off as the thief attempted to offer alternative solutions. "There's still a wizard to vanquish and a princess to rescue."

He made his way over the dragon's tail and slid around it to the grand doors that she guarded. As if on cue, the twin doors swung open, revealing the dark decor of a magic themed throne room.

The throne was empty of the castle's owner, making the scene feel a little bare. Astral had stuck her head and most of her body through the doorway, and William cursed at her, unable to scale or squeeze his way past. He grunted as he tried to push her through the door.

Thunder rumbled outside, and lightning illuminated the tower that sat atop a spiral of tall, crumbling stairs as seen from a crumbled balcony that overlooked the overgrown labyrinthine gardens below. The princess wasn't much further. Seth shuddered. A loud snap, followed by a cloud of thick, colourful smoke, drew Seth's attention back to the throne room.

Maniacal laughter echoed around them, but Seth didn't feel the essence of evil behind it. As the smoke cleared, a lanky, pimply youth emerged while flailing his staff in a vain attempt to clear the air. He wore flamboyant robes with large sleeves, and a pointed large rimmed hat with bobbles dangling from each of its three curled ends.

Seth regarded the dragon. "Do you know this guy?"

Astral sniffed at the teen wizard. Surprised that the dragon was still alive, he thumped her snout with his gnarly homemade staff. One of its decorative charms hit the ground with a clang.

She recoiled, holding her sore snout, breaking the entrance to the throne room. She growled and slithered in, pouncing on the wizard. The wizard wet himself.

"You're supposed to be dead," he squeaked.

"I decided not to be," she growled, baring her sharp teeth.

"That's not part of the script!" He flailed his arm and legs from under the dragon's claw, hoping to squirm his way free. "You're not following the script!"

"You want to know what else isn't in the script?"

The wizard's eyes bulged as she pressed down on him a little.

"You'll give me your hat," she told him.

He stared up at her large dragon eyes. "Yes, take the hat!" he cried out. She let him go and placed the hat on her head, opting to hang it off one of her horns, as the wizard hid behind Seth and pointed up at her. "She's the wizard now! Beat her up!" Seth and Astral exchanged looks, sizing each other up.

"I think I'll pass on that one," Seth said.

"You have to! You're the hero and heroes beat up dragons!" the wizard screamed.

Astral's tongue was inspecting the space between one of her teeth. Seth regarded her once more just as she freed the piece of meat and brought it up to eye level for closer inspection.

"Oh, come on, she's hardly threatening," Seth tried to reason with the wizard.

In a sudden surge of courage, the wizard pulled up his sleeves and stormed toward the dragon, who stopped what she was doing to watch him. "The joke's on you!" the wizard said. "That's a cursed hat!"

"Oh no!" Astral sounded genuinely concerned. She pulled the hat from her horn to inspect it. "No one likes a cursed hat. What's it do? Does it have fleas? I hate fleas!"

"It'll turn you into a human!" he roared. Seth considered for a moment that, while she may have been intimidating as a dragon, she was still a threat to the wizard, even in human form.

She studied the hat once again. In a show of bright lights, she shrunk down to human size. Her scales melted away into her porcelain skin and wrapped her in fine black robes. She forced the hat over her wild ebony hair, where it immediately flopped to one side, and glared from beneath it. "It's still my hat!"

The wizard gaped. With his finger still pointing at the maiden, he blurted, "How'd that happen!?"

"Cursed hat, remember?" Seth replied. Then to Astral, as he moved to guide her away from the lanky teen, "Look on the bright side, you can fit through doors!"

"But my nest." She sulked. "The gold will be too hard to sleep on now."

"Oh, I'm sure we can find a use for the gold," he offered.

"I don't want to sleep on the ground! It's undignified."

"I suppose you could try out something a little softer?"

"Seth!" The voice grated on his nerves. He couldn't help but cringe as Nicole dashed out from a passage hidden in the pillar nearest to the wall, with William in tow. Seth noted that the stairs to the passage must have been hidden behind one of the decorative drapes hanging from the buttress.

"Oh, my hero has come at last!" Nicole swooned, throwing herself into Seth's arms. Her costume was a tight leotard with a deep V-neck that reveal her ample assets. She had a shimmering transparent skirt and high-heeled shoes. A tiara had been securely attached to her stiff blonde hair. "I ask nothing more than for you to take me to my father." She breathed each line like it was her last sultry breath.

Seth looked to Astral, who smiled deviously in return. He smirked down at the princess, who was about to reach up to kiss him, and said, "I'm afraid not, Princess." And with that, he spun her out of his arms to fall into William's.

William looked at Nicole and smiled. "I'll rescue you, Princess."

"And deliver this message to your father," Seth added, "the next princess who sacrifices a dragon to get a husband will find herself very disappointed."

Nicole pushed her way out of William's struggling arms and stormed toward the hero. "Look here Seth, you have no idea who you're messing with! I can make your life a living hell!" she screeched.

"And so the princess was rescued, and they all lived happily ever after," the director's voice boomed from above, ending the play. Music filled the air as the cast and castle vanished from sight.

Seth's pod cracked open, allowing a rush of cool air to greet him. He hadn't realized how hot he'd been. He glanced down at his shirt, finding it torn and stained with blood. The events in the play were meant to be theatrical; no one was supposed to get hurt. His stomach twisted as he considered the dragon's fate had he chosen to follow the script.

He exited the auditorium with the rest of the students. Nicole pushed him as he entered the dressing area. "What the hell did you think you were doing!? Siding with that freak!" she bellowed.

Seth glanced over his shoulder, admiring the shade of red she had turned. "Can you get to the point?" he said. One of his wounds had opened up and he could feel blood trickling down his skin. He needed to get to the healer before the injury got infected.

Nicole was flustered. "You were going to have the best night of your miserable little life," she returned, thrusting a finger in his face.

"Miss, I wouldn't dream of dishonouring you in such a way, no matter how much you begged," Seth replied, pulling his cloak from his shoulders and walking away to the sound of Nicole swearing vengeance, amid snickering peers.

"I expected better of you!" the director shouted at Seth, pushing his way through the students in pursuit of the star. "You're an example to your peers."

Seth hesitated for a moment before grabbing the director by the arm and pulling him through the masses to a quieter area. "You see these?" he hissed, pressing the director's hand against his bleeding wounds. "This is real blood!" He forced the director's clammy hand up to his face to better see the colour.

"Now, think about what kind of example I would have set had I killed Astral," he hissed. He could feel the venom bubbling inside of him. If he had killed her, he would never have forgiven himself.

"Think about how that would have made me look!" He grabbed the director by the shirt. "I would have been publicly exposed as a bigot. My future with the Council would have been ruined. Now, think about who would have to pay the price for that," he growled.

Seth pushed the director away. No one would know just how close they had been to danger that night. As he made his way to the infirmary, he wondered if he should tell Astral.

She would want to find the source and deal with it before it got out of hand. As the healer came in, he decided that he would investigate on his own. At least then, Astral could walk away with a positive experience; he would shoulder the weight of knowing that someone out there had tried to kill them.

STORY III

ARCANUM MUTATIO

ARCANUM MUTATIO

Summer had been good to the small village of Clearwater. The farms were thriving, which meant that it would be a prosperous year for its citizens. They attributed their good fortune to the Red Order's Hunters, who had kept the number of demonic incidents at a record low.

In fact, the incident reports hadn't been this low since Adora Mathers, the village's unofficial spokesperson, was alive some fifteen years prior. Since her death, the people had agreed to allow the Red Order to erect their temple in a heavily wooded area north of the village as long as their Demon Hunters protected them.

Mathias Mathers was now the unofficial spokesperson for the village and a Master Hunter of the Red Order. And, like his mother before him, he patrolled the area every night without asking for a single credit.

It was on one such night that Mathias's son, William, broke into his father's study.

The Master Hunter had moved boxes of old world manuscripts and antiquities from around the house into his private study when the teen had arrived home from the Academy.

The Order often dropped off materials for his father's inspection, and growing up, William had become accustomed to his father's lengthy periods of studying in isolation. This time it was different. He had never questioned his father's work, never once thought to ask what it was for. He figured if he did, he'd be put to work, forced to spend the summer transcribing notes.

But William had learned over his school year that the Red Order often obtained books of a questionable nature. His friends theorized that the contents of such books were taboo or black magic.

Wanting to share the mystery of his father's work, William had divulged the details to Seth, a schoolmate who had graduated that year. Seth was three years older than William, who, a few short weeks ago, had celebrated his fifteenth birthday.

Magic, Seth had reasoned, was often the default response to explain away the unknown. Labelling materials as "black magic" exemplified the ignorance and irrational mind of the people who had given it that title.

William wanted to prove Seth wrong, magic did exist, but he needed to get into his father's study before Astral Daamon arrived for her summer stay. Astral was his childhood friend. He had known her ever since he first moved to Clearwater. This past year though, he couldn't stand the thought of her.

He had learned of her family's dark history and had chosen his allies carefully, while Seth took pity on her, allowing her to hang out with him.

William thought it was rather pathetic of her to follow Seth around like some pet. Though she'd be hard-pressed for friends next year, since Seth had sworn his Oath and would be sent to the war front.

William fiddled with the lock mechanism on the study door, ear pressed to the wood. He had taken every opportunity to work on picking the lock since his return home, which had proved to be easier than expected. Mathias had a love of the old and hadn't replaced the locks with the technological safeguards offered by the city. He didn't see the point in focusing on keeping people out of rooms when his real concern was to keep the demons out of the house.

Click went the lock, and with a final twist on the handle, the door creaked open, revealing the cluttered mess that was Mathias's workspace. In the darkness, William relied on the light filtering in from the hall to make out the contents of the room. Stacked to the ceiling, boxes took up a large part of the study; the pile would shrink over the summer, giving the room more breathing space. There was a narrow path to the desk that sat next to the window.

William dashed across the room to close the curtains, hoping to block any light from reaching the outside world. He made a mental note to return them to their original state before he left, even if it was in haste.

He ambled from box to box, debating which one to open, which book to riffle through. Overall, nothing jumped out at him. It all looked so boring, so old. He bent over the nearest box that lay open.

William pulled an old book from the box and looked it over. The binding was coming apart, and the cover had long lost its sheen. He flipped through the book looking for some illustrations to pique his interest and found none. Judging by the length of many of the words, it was probably a book on some old science.

There were several volumes of the same style. The language was old; some lettering, though familiar, was difficult to understand. He guessed that these were here for translation work to reveal what the world was like before the demon invasion.

At school, William learned that much of the world's history had been lost over the past couple of hundred years. He just found it hard to believe that one day all the databanks mysteriously crashed and that the people forgot everything. It was too much of a coincidence.

William moved on to another box. Another set of books, but these were older. He could see that the books had been maintained over the years. He riffled through the contents of the book, revealing handwritten passages and diagrams. The language was impossible to understand, but the pictures told a story.

He settled on an image of a man, arms and legs spread out. The man was surrounded by three circles with a series of symbols; William guessed that they represented the names of each ring. In the smallest ring containing the man, was an inverted triangle. In each point of the triangle was a glyph. The glyphs depicted the faces of a bear, wolf, and eagle

Before he could study them any further, William heard the front door open, followed by the sound of his father entering, dropping his gear and closing the door behind him.

William didn't waste any time. He tore the page from the book, stuffing it into his back pocket, opened the curtains and, in a few long strides, covered the space from the desk to the hall. He shut the door behind him and tested it to see if it was locked again.

Satisfied, he steadied his breathing and prepared to play off his presence outside the study, as his father would be on his way up, when he heard a second, unfamiliar voice downstairs.

"I apologize for the short notice, Mathias," said the voice. William walked down the staircase to see an older gentleman standing inside the entrance of the house. He wore a fine coat, advertising that he was a man of stature. He was older than he sounded, with neat grey hair, a trimmed beard, and deep age lines covering his face.

Next to him stood a bald man in a black uniform and sunglasses. William thought everything about the man radiated "cool". Especially the way he stood solid like a wall, emanating strength and durability. He knew that this bald man was the old guy's bodyguard and wondered if there were more patrolling the area.

William entered the room with a casual hello, breaching their private bubble.

Then he saw her. Shoulder length ebony hair and piercing blue eyes set in a fair-skinned face. Astral was taller than William by two inches without the help of any heeled shoes. She wore the clothes of an upper-class city dweller, whose preference lay in practicality instead of fashion, which had the effect of making her appear to be far too serious for her age.

Tonight, and upon her departure home, would be the only time she would wear such expensive clothes. Because of her frequent stays, Mathias had seen fit to keep a spare wardrobe full of the local fashions that he felt were suitable for a girl her age.

"What are you doing here?" William blurted out loudly.

"Training," she replied. Her voice was sharp and her tone condescending, as though she was speaking to a subordinate. She was good at keeping their communication short, and William always found it hard to tell what she was thinking behind that crystalline gaze.

He grimaced. "Dad," he turned to Mathias, "you've got to be kidding me. How come we always get landed with her?"

William thought he looked nothing like his father. Mathias was six feet tall, in his early thirties, with a head of dark brown hair and soulful brown eyes. He had a solid build in contrast to his son's lanky structure. William was always told that he had his mother's looks.

Dezmond, the older gentleman, arched a brow as he regarded the young man. He glanced at his granddaughter who, while mirroring his expression, seemed far more amused by her rude play-fellow.

"I apologize for the inconvenience, Mathers," Dezmond finally said, "I will see to other arrangements for next year. However, my expertise is required and I cannot compromise my granddaughter's safety."

He regarded Astral once more. Her slight smile betrayed the underlying playfulness in her nature. Dezmond decided to indulge her, turning to William. "I'll tell you what. For your inconvenience, I shall pay you a sum of two credits per day."

"You're paying me to be friends with her?" William said, surprised by his good fortune. He couldn't wait to tell everyone at the Academy.

Dezmond smiled. "Oh, heaven's no! I trust that you have far more integrity than that. I expect that my granddaughter will return to me in good condition and her reputation intact."

William considered this. This meant that he could only get paid if he didn't tell anyone that Astral had to pay people to be her friends. He reasoned that he could wait until he saw his schoolmates in the Autumn term. As though sensing this, and having been a clever young man himself at one time, Dezmond added, "The contract stipulates that no one is to know that she was here, meaning that, should you tell after you are paid, the credits will be refunded. Are we in agreement?"

William's thoughtful expression turned sour. "Make it ten credits and you have a deal."

"Eight," Dezmond challenged.

"Deal!" He shook the old man's hand to consummate their deal. He could feel his father's gaze burning into the side of his face; William hadn't thought for a second that his father babysitting the granddaughter of a Councilman might have been beneficial to their family. It was something that he would not reflect upon for several years to come.

Dezmond turned to Mathias. "You will train her in the areas I have requested." Though the statement had the ring of a question, Mathias had no choice. He nodded once. There was a trace of doubt in his eyes.

William wondered if little miss perfect had met a challenge in her training regiment as a demon hunter. With that, Dezmond kissed his granddaughter's forehead and bade her goodbye. Astral thought the action was more of a formality and she did not return the sentiment, much to her grandfather's dismay.

He left without another word.

Ⅎ)ℭ

That night, William sat up in bed staring at the torn page. He wondered about the hidden meaning of the symbols and flipped the page to inspect the handwriting, to see if he could make out any familiar letters that might form words. He tried for the better part of the night before eventually falling asleep.

His thoughts infiltrated his dreams, shaping a world of possibilities. Three bright purple rings hovered around him, each one larger than the next. Around the last ring orbited a tall wall of glyphs.

In this dream, he knew what each one meant. He knew that to achieve a transformation into the creature he desired, the sequence mattered.

"William!" his father's voice called into the dream world. "Get down here before breakfast is gone!"

William scowled and forced himself from his dream state.

His body resented being awake. He wiped the drool from his face and sat up to get ready for the day ahead, but as he did, the soft ruffling sound of paper drew his attention. Somewhere beneath the folds of his blanket, the page had lodged itself.

He pulled it free, inspecting it once more before folding it and sliding it between his mattresses.

If he didn't hurry, their guest would eat his share of the food.

❧⟡❧

Training started after breakfast. Mathias had a large list of skills and techniques to teach his Hunting apprentice before her grandfather returned. He used to have a whole summer to teach her the required materials. After the Enhanced fiasco at the Academy last year, Astral had restricted outings from her hometown, Serenity. This year he didn't have the time to work at a slower pace, which would have benefited his newly apprenticed son.

William's apprenticeship had happened by accident. He had been watching the summer lessons between his father and Astral for many years now and picked up some fighting techniques. In the periods when he was alone, he practiced with the dull training weapons, which were only available when she stayed with them.

Until this past year, his father had ignored him, but after William passed the apprenticeship exam, Mathias had to acknowledge that perhaps his son wasn't as useless as he thought.

Hunting had never particularly appealed to William, but it seemed like the general population liked it. Since becoming his father's apprentice, he had attracted a great deal of attention from his peers. Yet he longed for more. He had spent years living in Seth's shadow. Next year, he would finally be free to make his own mark at the Academy without hearing Seth's name being whispered by the students. Girls wanted Seth's attention and boys wanted to be him because of it. William was no different in this respect.

As far as apprenticeship lessons went, they were duller than he had imagined. That morning, their modest backyard had been cleared of outdoor furniture, while the tall fence did its best to block out curious eyes from peering in on the lesson.

"Clear your mind and focus," Mathias instructed. "Let all thoughts melt away. Listen only to the sound of your breathing."

The apprentices sat across from their master, mimicking his position, legs folded underneath them, arms resting on their knees. They sat in silence, eyes closed, breathing in a slow and steady rhythm as they focused on Mathias's voice.

The world melted away for William. He sensed Astral near him and his father across from him, but before long, his companions vanished from his imagination, leaving him in a place of complete stillness. He could no longer hear his father's voice, the voice that he so often sought to block out. Retreating inside of himself was the only way that he could manage it so completely.

He felt that these meditation sessions were a complete waste of time. What did clarity have to do with fighting a demon head-on? What mattered was being able to keep your head when you saw one.

He figured he'd entertain himself for a while and take the time to think back to his dream. He conjured an image of the clues he'd dreamed up, imagining a ring of fire around him. Fire made him feel strong, dominant. Only the strong could tame fire and bend it to their will.

He visualized himself tracing what he remembered of the glyphs into the air. The first glyph flashed and seared the surrounding air, reappearing outside of the ring of fire, the conjurer's circle. He traced the remaining two, each reappearing in the corners of the invisible triangle.

As though obeying a command, the fire rose around him and swallowed him whole. In a moment of panic, everything went black.

ಬೊೀಞ

William woke on the ground in a strange forest not of this world. A cool breeze broke the humidity, and the branchless trees welcomed the breeze with a dance. The trees were towering, flexible pillars. Beneath him, the ground was pink with the occasional black blotchy patch.

William got up and shook himself off. He didn't feel right in his body. It moved all wrong. He swayed as he tried to steady himself, leaning against the base of a tree. He looked down at four of his six legs, but he couldn't quite put his finger on what was different. He looked at his hands, which were now two more matching black legs. As he inspected them, he tried to remember what wasn't right with what he was seeing.

Something in the back of his mind panicked. Through hundreds of insect eyes, he took in the world around him. The skies were clear, no shadows on the ground. He wondered if demons could reach him here. Or perhaps he was in a demon world.

Fear took over, but the fear wasn't his. It was as though he was feeling the intense emotions of another person. A predator was near, the other person in his mind observed. He began to run in long leaps and bounds, his body controlled by the other presence. He fled his fear in long leaps, bounding so high that he saw nothing but a sea of green surrounding his island. From the seas rose massive wooden structures. Overhead the sun flickered through a canopy of jade clouds. It seemed familiar somehow.

He could not escape his fear. He felt an unseen predator in constant pursuit of him, and the growing intensity of his panic overwhelmed him. By the time he took his last great leap into the emerald sea, he was already unconscious.

₭)ℒ

William gasped, free of his meditative trance. His muscles ached as though he hadn't moved in hours. It was mid-afternoon, judging by the way the light hit the garden. He must have fallen asleep during the session.

His father and Astral weren't with him. At this time of the day, they were probably off on some trail, tracking potential nesting grounds. William was relieved to be left behind. These expeditions were uneventful and ended as glorified hiking exercises.

He considered taking the time to catch up with some friends and maybe sneak down to the town and back before they got home. Even if they got back before he did, he could always claim that he was out looking for them.

Realizing that he had hours to himself, William thought he'd try his father's study again and get a better look at the book's other illustrations.

When he opened the door, he found his father's study tidy. There were a few boxes lining the wall by the window, but most of them had gone from the room.

He wondered if his father had moved them or if the Red Order had come while he was meditating. It was strange to walk into the almost empty room, when only the night before it had barely enough room to breathe in. He knew his father was good at what he did, but he never imagined that he could get through those translations so fast. Unless he wasn't doing translation work...

Why move everything upstairs if the Red Order were collecting it today? Too many questions that would remain unanswered.

The room itself was a soft shade of blue, complemented with white mouldings. Covering the far wall, there was an antique glass cabinet with long drawers at its base. The cabinet was locked, safeguarding a series of old catalogues and holographic family portraits. As he glanced around, William recognized his older sister, who had passed away when he was four. There were others standing with her, faces he didn't recognize. There was a man in a red robe – a sign of his allegiance and of his rank within the Order. An older woman stood at his side. Her posture and neat clothing and hair suggested that she was a refined and respectable woman. There were other objects in the display case, none of which held William's interest.

He checked through the remaining boxes, none of which had the book he had discovered last night. He was disappointed, but not surprised. There was something about the whole experience that made him feel as though he was meant to find that book. He believed that there was a reason he was drawn to that specific page.

‽

William woke when he heard the front door close. He glanced at the clock in the top corner of the tablet that lay open on his chest. Messages between friends remained open on the screen, though each conversation had long since ended.

He must have fallen asleep. He didn't remember feeling tired. It had been mid-afternoon when he was checking on his friends. Now it was close to three in the morning.

"William," his father called. He didn't sound happy. William heard Mathias climbing the stairs. He knocked, as was his habit, before peering into his son's room. William pretended to sleep. It was unlikely that his father would tear him out of bed to ream him for whatever he had or hadn't done. They had a guest, not that Astral hadn't had front row seats to one of their fights in the past.

Besides, Mathias avoided dealing with his son whenever he could. At this late hour he was probably more interested in sleep than reprimanding William. William heard the gentle click of his bedroom door latch shut, and Mathias's calm stride grow distant as he settled into his late night routine.

‽

Every day for the next week, right after breakfast, they proceeded with their meditation session. William used this time to try to rebuild the image from the book in his mind, instead of focusing on the intended lesson. He struggled, failing to return to the dark, isolated place where he could drown out his father's voice.

At one point, he got as far as summoning the first of the three rings, but every time he tried to add the second ring, his mind resisted. He struggled to maintain his mental hold over the image in his mind, feeling the rings shrink and expand with a will of their own. It wasn't long into these frustrating experiences that William realized that his imaginings were very real.

He focused his mind and let the world slip away, leaving himself alone to build the first ring as he done without issue during his previous sessions. He envisioned a brilliant fiery halo as the second ring that rose into position. The second ring kept rising, refusing to remain level with the first ring.

William tried to slam the third ring in place before the second ring drifted outside his attention, and became too difficult to hold its shape with his limited imagination.

His frustration mounted.

William reaffirmed the first circle that had erased itself when he acknowledge the disappearance of the second ring. In quick succession, he called onto several heavy rings to fall into the second position, hoping that the weight of his will would hold his haloed ring in place. He carved the third ring into the earth of his imaginary world.

He felt his imagination resist, wanting to undo itself. He pushed on, calling on the rings faster and harder, wedging his desires into position. When all three rings existed in full, the images shattered.

William jumped as the invisible shards cut him. The sensation of tiny fragments against his skin was just enough to distract from the dull burning that he felt on his face and hands. Inspection following a similar incident earlier that week had revealed that the burns could not be seen, but he'd felt their slow throbbing for days.

He realized too late that he had drawn his father's attention. Mathias looked annoyed.

"This is stupid!" William shouted in frustration. He wanted to hide his minor injuries. He didn't want his father to learn that he had been going through the volumes in his private study. Most of all, he didn't want to be reported to the Red Order for archaic crimes which would, in these days, mark him as Enhanced.

It terrified him.

"Finding your center is a part of your training," Mathias said, having been in William's position in his youth. "It will help you think rationally when you are facing impossible odds."

William chanced a glance at Astral, who carried on ignoring him. She was such a goody-goody. Her ease with the exercise made him just that much more frustrated with himself. It led him to think of Seth. With all of his expertise, did he have to spend his mornings meditating?

"Instincts, while critical to a Hunter, aren't enough when it comes to dispatching a demon," his father continued.

"When do we get to learn some moves?" William thrust his arms out and flailed them around in a sloppy imitation of the karate moves that he had seen his fellow students show off.

Mathias rolled his eyes and stood up. He stopped his son from acting out by placing his hands on his shoulders, grounding his senses. He towered over William, making him feel like he was six years old again.

William had the notion that children should feel safe around their parents, but his father's presence always made him feel uncomfortable, as though he was being stalked by a predator who was only biding his time.

"Honestly, William, the bulk of Hunting is research and tracking. The action part of it doesn't last long at all, and to survive that you need to be in a state of complete clarity. It's the key to becoming a skilled Hunter." Mathias tried to impart his knowledge.

"Like Seth?" William asked.

Mathias hesitated. He turned to Astral and patted her on the head, signalling the end of the session. Protocol would have had him ease her out of the meditative state, but given William's outburst, he figured she had already been pulled back to reality and chose to remain uninvolved.

"Seth's feats have been remarkable for one so young," Mathias admitted. "However, given that I am not his Master, I can't say with any certainty that meditation is as much a part of his daily routine as it is ours."

"So why can't I be trained by his Master instead?" William retorted.

"Because Seth doesn't have a Master," Astral replied on Mathias's behalf. He would have preferred if his apprentice had not mentioned that part.

"Then I don't need one either," William announced.

"If you want to work for the Red Order you do," Mathias said.

"Who says that I want to work for the Order?" His son dismissed the idea.

"It's tradition," Mathias said. He wasn't sure if his son was being serious, though if he was it would come as a huge relief. Mathias's father had been an esteemed devotee of the Faith and had, during his formidable years, established religious centers within many of the remaining surface towns, until he reached Clearwater, where its citizens had denied the Red Order a place of worship.

It was also the place where his father had met his mother, Adora, where they had married, and where he, Mathias, was born. The same place where his father met his early death at the hands of a wraith.

Yet, the Red Order made heavy demands of it's practitioners, robbing its flock of all semblance of free will. William would work the jobs he was told to work. He would move the backwatered towns that he deemed unworthy of him in order to teach him humiliation. A wife would be chosen for him, but only after he proved a worthy Hunter. He would own nothing, but he would be provided for based on what he gave to the Order. A personality like William's could do a great deal of harm to society if he succeeded within the organizations ranks.

"That's a lame reason to do something," Astral said. Mathias scowled, wishing that she were less confident to voice such strong opinions. If he were oblivious of her history, he'd have blamed youthful ignorance. Her words cut deep, forcing him to consider the hidden meaning of her statement. She valued traditions and rituals herself, as long as it had a purpose.

William's exposure to the world of the Red Order did not make him an exceptional candidate for the priesthood. Tradition in this case, reduced the boy's learning curve and the effort needed to indoctrinate him into their way of thinking. Perhaps she had a point. Still, he wished she'd keep her opinions to herself.

"What do you know," William spat, "Your father was a traitor and a murderer."

"My father wasn't a murderer," Astral growled, narrowing her eyes.

"William, that's enough," Mathias snapped. "Since you feel that you have surpassed my teachings, feel free to be elsewhere. I have another apprentice to train."

William felt that he was being brushed aside, that he wasn't worth arguing with. He stormed off, fuming that his father didn't care one way or another about his training.

Back inside, he slammed the door to his room. He had mixed feelings about this turn of events. While he wanted out of the boring meditation sessions, he didn't want to end his training all together. He wanted to have something to show off to his friends at school, a few cool combos that could cement his candidacy as a skilled demon killer. He couldn't just very well sit there in a trance. He'd be laughed out of the school.

Though he didn't want an audience to his meditative failings, he did want the time to figure out the spell from the book. Not that using magic at school was wise, even if he did get it to work. Mastering the spell would be something unique to him.

Truth was, he had yet to prove himself against a real demon.

He couldn't just say that he had killed one, especially since both Astral and Seth had killed their demons publicly. Astral would never have qualified under the Red Order's stringent induction requirements otherwise.

William didn't see his first demon until last year. Even then, it wasn't a real demon. The Red Order had used some old testing program to see how candidates reacted in the face of death. He ran.

No, he couldn't afford to give up on his training, even if he felt that it wasn't going anywhere. His best alternative would be to seek another master or get training in the areas he felt would help him.

Sighing, he picked up his tablet and checked over his messages, responding to some. His finger hovered over Seth's name for a moment as he debated whether he should say anything at all. Would it hurt to ask? Would he agree to train William? Would he share his secrets?

William wondered if Astral communicated with Seth at all. He considered sneaking up to her room to see if he could find her tablet. If he found it, he could pretend to be her and send Seth a message on his behalf. It would make things easier.

He'd have to wait until they left the house before he tried it. In the meantime...

He pulled the page from between his mattresses and inspected it for the hundredth time that week. He scrutinized every detail. It was the reason he'd tried to add two extra rings during his meditation instead of sticking with just the one. There had to be a significance to it, even though it felt easier to handle one ring.

Lying down flat on his back, he tucked the paper away after one last inspection. He would try again.

His world melted away with every breath, leaving an image of himself alone in the void where anything was possible. The first ring came into being in a show of flames, leaving behind an ever-burning fiery circle. He felt in control.

Next came the second circle. Focusing on the space a few feet outside of the first ring, he pictured flames ripping through the emptiness, until it closed in on itself, sealing the second ring as imagined flames shot skyward before settling into glowing embers. Beads of sweat dotted his brow as he concentrated on keeping the embers of the first circle burning.

The images he called to mind should have been easy, and yet he struggled with these basic shapes. He had his hands full with these two and he would have to let go of one to conjure the final circle. His control was slipping. He had to act fast. He decided against placing the third ring.

Instead, he called the glyphs. He had spent a great deal of time memorizing the pattern of each one.

The glyphs changed form quickly and of their own free will. It was like watching the numbers on a roulette wheel whiz by, and William was just as helpless to will it to choose his chosen symbol. William forced the frustration from his mind and waited for the symbol to self-select. The spell chose a series of triangular glyphs with curled features. Where those wings? Was that a rams head or rat? The glyphs changed as though searching for viable options. Did the spell have a will of its own?

As the thought occurred to William, the dull shimmering glyphs lit up in unison, and everything went black.

₧)(Ω

When William regained consciousness, he first noticed the sensation of strong winds against his face. He felt like he was falling into the darkness of his inner mind. He flailed, grabbing at nothing, screaming. In a bright pulse, he saw the world around him.

The shock of the vision silenced him. Then, just as fast as it had come, his vision was gone.

The sense that he was falling hadn't left him. If he didn't do something soon, he would end up as a smear on the hard surface below. Instinct took over, as though he had a co-pilot watching from the back of his mind.

He flapped his arms together to force his body into an upright position, hoping to catch a strong current that would take him higher. For a moment, he enjoyed the freedom of flying.

Until something crashed into him. Furious claws and fangs bit into his arms and legs. He could've sworn that whatever it was even cursed at him. The pain forced him from the experience.

ഇൽ

William gasped. For a half second, the dark world around him was foreign. He remembered that he was in his room and sat up, opening the window, drawn to the skies. As he looked over the lush forests beyond the village, he could make out a family of bats starting their night-time feast.

It felt too real to be a dream.

A knock at the door drew his attention. Three solid raps in succession meant that Astral was at the door. "Dinner is ready," she called. "We're heading out on patrol afterwards if you want to come along."

Once she left at the end of the week, hunting demons would become a lesser priority in William's training – he still had a lot of basics to cover. It was best to take part in the hunt while he could.

Fatigue gnawed at his bones as he made his way down to the kitchen. He wondered if he had the energy to last a full late-night patrol. The smell of cooked meat sharpened his mind, and his stomach growled.

He sat down heavily in his seat at the table. Without inspecting what Mathias had prepared, he began throwing assorted food items onto his plate while shovelling whatever he could into his mouth.

One perk of living on the surface was that it was easier to get fresh food, and for Red Order Hunters its availability was guaranteed; they wouldn't have to endure the food supplements that the city provided.

Mathias could only watch in horrified silence as his son devoured his meal at an alarming rate. While Astral looked on in amusement, hiding her knowing smile behind a bun.

William caught the smile and swallowed hard. "What are you looking at?" he snapped, terrified that she knew for certain what he was only beginning to suspect.

Without saying a word, she placed a second slice of meat onto his plate and observed. He stared down at the morsel, watching its juices bathe his untouched vegetables. Its savoury smell called to him and his body obeyed the call. He wanted to deny it; he wanted to resist. He knew, even as he took another serving of meat, that she knew that he had stumbled upon something special, something that was changing him. He was becoming a mage.

Astral stole William's vegetables and relinquished her portion of protein in such a casual way that the ravenous boy didn't even notice.

William finished dinner too fast, and while their house guest had eaten a healthy share, unbothered by her peer's sudden spike in appetite, Mathias hadn't touched his meal. His fork sat by his plate as he contemplated.

"You will not be joining us tonight," he said at last, "it's best that you get your rest." William hadn't expected such a compassionate tone from his father.

⁎

William woke to find Astral standing over his bed in full battle gear. The gleam in her crystalline stare shone in the moonlight. She seemed less than human, a demon in a young woman's skin.

He felt the sweat beading on his forehead.

"Whatever it is you are doing, you will stop," she told him.

He snarled, insulted that she would rob him of his new power. "Where do you get off?" he barked.

She stared down at him and he fell silent. "I'll not bother with a lecture. Now give me the spell."

Inside he could feel a sense of victory wash over him. At least one rumour was true about the Red Order. They had old magic in their possession. "I don't know what you're talking about, freak!" He hoped that he was making enough noise to draw his father's attention.

He expected her to pull him from his bed. He expected to see the sheen of her blue eyes ignite in a savage rage. He expected to have the shadows come down on him and tear him to shreds. Yet all that happened was that she blinked at him and cocked her head.

He didn't know why he'd imagined such a horrifying display. Still, he could almost hear his blood splattering against the walls of his room and smell his blood wetting his mattress.

"I'll tell on you," she said at last.

His heart sank to his stomach. If she told the Order, they'd kill him on the spot. "You wouldn't," he hissed.

She blinked at him again. He felt idiotic; Astral would most certainly tell on him, she was a do-gooder. He reached for the parchment between his sheets and handed it over.

She glanced at it, flipped it over as though to make sure that everything was there, and then walked away without saying another word.

They didn't speak to each other for the rest of the week. William wondered if Astral had played his fears against him.

When Astral left, normality resumed in the Mathers household. The training sessions stopped, since William made a big deal about wanting to spend time with friends this summer, which left him with a lot more time on his hands. He spent the better part of his days showing off for the locals with some of his cooler fighting moves he had learn from Seth while at school.

He couldn't do this with Astral around. She'd probably show him up or lecture him about showing off. It had been over a month since she was in Clearwater, yet he was still angry with her. Until suddenly it occurred to him that although she had the physical version of the spell, he had memorized it.

One afternoon, William decided to prove to himself that he didn't need the page to perform the spell.

He sat beneath a willow tree on the outskirts of town, in place where he knew the villagers were too afraid to wander unless dared on the darkest of nights. As he concentrated on his breathing, his last thoughts were of Astral. Hurt and rage flooded his mind, but instead of allowing it to wreak havoc, he refocused it. "I'll show her what I'm capable of."

If he could master this spell, he would have the power to transform into whatever beast he could think up. This could be his thing. This could be his contribution to the world as his own unique brand of Hunter.

Astral didn't understand how important it was for him to be useful.

As he sank deeper into the motions of the spell, he felt his spirit soar into the sky and fly across the countryside at lightspeed. His spirit plunged into the ground, fixated on an unseen source of energy that called to him. He could not disobey.

☙❧

William woke to darkness. He pulled himself up from the spot where he had collapsed just moments prior. His brothers had gone ahead to deal with the threat that invaded their new home.

The copper scent of blood made him hungry, but that sweet treat was reserved for the hatchlings. He heard them, hundreds of tiny voices, calling for warmth, food and repositioning. He heard the brood mother's voice call out instructions to her children on how to navigate the labyrinth of caves; and to the drones, orders to tend to the children.

Just as he felt her inspecting his mind, he lost his connection with her – only for a moment, but it was enough to cause concern. He heard her internal struggle: *Be rid of the weak link or use him as a shield.*

Either way, today he would die.

He would protect the nest. This is what he was born to do. He ran through the labyrinth, using his mind-link with the other drones to guide him. His race did not see, not in the traditional sense. He saw the world in sounds, in the vibration of every step, with each texture and with each taste.

He was connected to everything that mattered. He could feel their happiness, their hunger, their pleasure, and their pain. The intruder had killed a number of his brothers, who hadn't heard them coming but felt the cold metal tear through their thick skin.

There was no fear, though. Fear could be infectious and, therefore, was a forbidden emotion. Only the young were allowed to be afraid. Anyone beyond that was executed.

Again, the cool caress of steel sliced through him as another hundred family members were slain. His brothers' blood did not smell as succulent as that of the warm-blooded creatures, and a bitter, potent stench spread through the caves they called home.

Then came the sound of light, hurried steps, followed by a pause. A loud thud echoed around him as the creatures hit the ground, and a hot and cold sensation filled his mind as another cluster of his brothers fell to the intruder.

They needed to coordinate their attacks if they were going to survive. They needed a clear image of their surroundings, to focus on their attacker. He issued the order to listen. His brothers who obeyed the command would no doubt perish. Their lives were worthy of sacrifice if it saved their young.

There it was, shallow, barely there. It seemed familiar somehow. She had to breathe when she executed her attack, but only just. It was enough to track her. With enough of his brothers around, he could sacrifice one and use the others to take her out.

Two of his brothers grabbed onto her feet, interrupting her attack, and smashed her into the floor. She arched her body, catching the ground and redirecting the force of the impact to pull herself free. He heard metal scraping stone, revealing the image of a long scythe lifting in preparation for a powerful blow. With a swing of her weapon, the small army before her was cut by half before melting away seconds later.

'Astral,' he thought to himself attracting the brood mother's attention once more. The brood mother searched his mind to understand the new word. Demon Hunter. Killer. Assassin. Danger. Images of human blood smeared against a human boy's wall, as he lay dying and bleeding in his own bed as an inhuman shadow loomed over him. She'd kill him for real if she knew what he had become.

Mother severed his connection from the rest of his family to avoid infection. He had seconds before Mother ended him herself. 'Mother,' he thought. 'I know this enemy. Let me handle her.'

A moment passed in silence. He was still alive, but he couldn't feel the hive mind of his siblings supporting him. He was alone. He knew from the paths that his brothers had already taken that Astral would have to come this way to face him. He had every intention of giving her the fight of her life.

He steadied his breathing and focused his thoughts, listening for the sound of her footsteps, light and purposeful as he had heard so many times in his home.

She stopped twenty feet in front of him – the heat of her weapon giving her position away.

He could hear the gears hidden inside of it click and grind. She could not unleash another disintegrating shot for some time.

Now that she had stopped, he could see the weapon, but he couldn't see her. "There's something off with this one," she whispered.

He sensed a great void open up in the darkness, giving way to the infinity stretching beyond it. He felt exposed and insignificant as the void grew and engulfed him. Eternity surrounded him.

"He's possessed," she stated with certainty. Her voice was distant and yet it was all around him. He couldn't pinpoint her exact position anymore, though he could feel her unwinding time itself to peer into the past and future. If she got much further, she'd know who he was.

He wanted her out of his soul. He lunged in the direction where he had last felt her. The void closed up and her blade slashed his body as she dodged the attack. He spun before the scythe could bite too deep, driving his powerful arms toward her. He felt his attack connect with her body.

Cold steel pierced through his abdomen. Someone else was there with her. The blade twisted inside of him as his unseen assailant prepared to push the blade all the way through. Instinct took hold. He lashed out. He felt his body pull apart, shifting his organs and freeing the weapon before she inflicted critical damage.

His arm split into hundreds of pointed tendrils and flailed for the unknown attacker. He could sense the scythe poised for another attack. Its heat signature fading but not gone. She had some time yet before she could use its long-range setting.

He twisted his body toward her and reshaped it in such a way that a large mouth formed. He screamed. The force of the sound sent the weapon and, he assumed, its mistress flying. He did not hear her hit the ground or any part of the cave walls.

He reshaped both arms into hundreds of jagged blades and sent them in the direction he assumed that she had fallen. He could just barely sense the scythe just outside the tunnel junction, hiding behind the rounded path. She was no doubt trying to get a sense for what waited for her beyond. "Take that, you cocky bitch!" he screamed. "Think you'll rat me out? I'll show you who's boss!"

His weapons drove into the wall behind the scythe, catching up the weapon itself. She wasn't there.

The cold steel sword slashed through him once more. In a moment he would die.

"William," a man growled. "I should have recognized your soul signature."

"Seth?" William could feel blood oozing from his body. "I didn't mean..." He was in agony. His body melting away. He willed it to remain. "I wanted to prove that I could help in other ways," he croaked. "I didn't want to hurt anyone."

"Shall I exorcise him?" Astral offered. The edge in her voice suggested that he would be better off dead.

"Please," he begged. "I should have left by now. It shouldn't have lasted this long. I don't understand. Please don't let me die."

He felt her hand on his face, and his instinct called out to him. He could deal one last blow and in doing so he could take her with him. William focused his mind, keeping the dying demon that he had possessed at bay. He was not the demon. He needed her to pull him out of the demon's body if he hoped to return to his own body sleeping beneath the willow tree.

A warm, bright light surrounded his dying body. The world melted away, leaving only himself in his demon form. As he drifted closer to the source of the light, it burned away the demon skin, revealing the frightened boy inside.

STORY IV

GUIDING LIGHT

GUIDING LIGHT

The township of Mountain Crest was brimming with excitement. A dozen handpicked students from the Council's Academy had chosen to visit as part of their historical tour, specifically to explore the Red Order monastery. Common folks were forbidden inside the place of worship, which made these children subject to local gossip and speculation.

On the day of their arrival, shop owners opened extra early, preparing special window displays and cleaning their storefronts to make them as inviting as possible, in the hope it would attract a wealthy patron or two. Handcrafted goods were all the rage in the capital, and some locals could do very well for themselves by meeting the demands of customers from the city.

The shuttle from the Council's Academy arrived a little before eight in the morning. Long, slender and oval in shape, it had a reflective metallic surface that tricked the demons into thinking nothing was there. If the curious few who had gathered in the square had dared to touch the machine, it would have felt cold. Even in the scorching conditions of the desert, this model's outer shell remained frigid, masking the heat signatures of those being transported inside.

There were no obvious windows or doors until, a few minutes after the quiet purr of the engine had stopped, a panel along the shuttle's side slid open, revealing an older woman.

Mrs. Price was the class instructor for the day and an avid historian, with a fondness for ancient architecture dated just after the official beginning of the Demon War, some two hundred years prior. She had soft brown eyes and a warm smile, that suited her rounded face and rounded figure. Her hair, wiry and grey, was cut in a heart shape.

Through exposure to the rich history of their ancestors, Mrs. Price hoped the students might understand that superiority had nothing to do with their survival into this new age. Having lived most of her life during the oppressive Military Regime, she wanted to close the gap between the surface world and those who lived safely in the underground sanctuary of the capital.

As she exited, Mrs. Price searched her surrounding for their first destination, and thus her first lesson for the day. One by one, the students filed out behind her, stretching after the two-hour journey.

This far north, winter still had a powerful hold over the region; the students had been advised to dress accordingly. Many of them wore coats that were fashionable but otherwise useless for the climate. A handful wore heavy, sensible coats, possibly because they were surface dwellers themselves. But one student took the warning of colder temperatures to an extreme.

Astral Daamon wore no less than three winter coats, four colourful hats, and three scarves wrapped around her head, nose, mouth, and neck, revealing only her piercing blue eyes. After much arguing about the school's dress code, she'd still had to wear her school uniform underneath, with the condition that she could add trousers. She even wore gloves beneath her bright red mitts.

The other students gave her a wide berth, afraid to acknowledge the eccentric fifteen-year-old who was striding in the direction of an aroma that promised delicious breakfast.

"This way," Mrs. Price called to her flock, leading them toward the restaurant.

Astral was speaking with the waitress by the time Mrs. Price and her class walked in. The waitress wore a white shirt and dark green skirt, and a long brown coat that fell to her ankles and fastened at her waist. She kept her long blond hair in a slender ponytail, which bobbed as she answered her patron's questions. The waitress, no older than the girl speaking to her, seemed distressed. She spoke rapid, hushed words, her green eyes darting about the room in case someone was watching them.

Astral nodded and turned to leave. The waitress grabbed her padded arm, but promptly let go as Astral's crystalline gaze met hers. After a moment, she looked away and proceeded with her work.

Mrs. Price urged her class to take their seats and settle into silence. She amused herself by watching the expressions on her students' faces as the mouth-watering aromas of cooked meats, eggs, toast and various apple, pear, and dried berry dishes spilled out from the kitchen. Stomachs growled. "Much of the produce that you enjoy at the Academy comes from these local farmers," she stated. "In fact, much of their food is consumed by the people in the capital city."

"Who doesn't get to eat?" Astral asked in her usual cold and direct fashion. She sat alone near the exit. Unlike her peers, she had remained in her winter gear.

Mrs. Price took a deep breath and smiled. Her colleagues had told her that this student was trouble with a capital T. That's not to say that many of the academic staff didn't like her. Several saw the potential in the young girl – one of whom was Mathias Mathers, a Master Hunter of the Red Order. He had requested that Miss Daamon join them on today's outing, feeling that she might enjoy an advanced class or two to keep her keen mind out of trouble.

"What do you mean, Astral?" Mrs. Price inquired warmly. She had counted on this student to ask the uncomfortable questions that most ignored.

"According to recent statistics, over eighty percent of the produce produced in any village is shipped to our capital, which leaves less than twenty percent to feed the village, and there's the Red Order's taxation, which takes another ten- to fifteen percent, depending on how they feel that year. It's reminiscent of the aristocracy, who would leave their people to starve, believing that they were expendable. My question is, at the expense of us eating, who in this village has to do without?" Astral explained.

Something was flung across the room and landed onto one of Astral's flamboyant hats. "If you have a problem with the way things are, freak, you can do without. Everyone knows that an Enhanced is just a waste of space anyway," one of her peers taunted.

The smile faded from Mrs. Price's face, somehow sapping the room of its hospitable warmth. The cruel laughter stopped.

"Miss Daamon brings up a valuable point." Mrs. Price regarded the assailant. "In exchange for the food, the city provides the locals with food cubes, which have all the nutrients the human body requires."

"That hardly seems fair," Astral retorted. "Have you ever eaten a food cube?" The girl squinted, no doubt part of a grimace that was hidden under her many scarves.

"Bet you have, loser!" her peer taunted again.

Mrs. Price held up her hand. "That's another legitimate question. Have any of you ever eaten a food cube?"

Silence lingered over the class. The instructor nodded and went away to speak with the proprietor. A moment later, a small handmade basket was brought out, filled with small, silver-wrapped cubes.

The waitress placed three cubes in front of each of the twelve students.

Astral slipped hers into her pocket to eat later.

It was the perfect form of torture to force these elitists to eat the sub-standard food cubes, while the intoxicating scent of real food hung in the air. Astral had no doubts she'd get blamed and would suffer the consequences of this little turn of events for the rest of her career as a student.

A chime sounded from her pocket and she pulled the pen-shaped tool from her coat, dropping it into her instructor's waiting hand. Her classmates watched in glee. The nib flashed a bright red, signalling that an important message was waiting.

Mrs. Price stared at the communicator in her hand before cracking open the device, splitting it in two, lengthwise, and studying the electronic feed that flashed across a thin panel on one side. *Dezmond.*

"Your grandfather," Mrs. Price said to Astral, handing back the tool.

"I told him about the trip last night," her student lied. "He's probably just worried." Astral regarded the message for a moment, as though considering her options, then asked to be excused. Permission granted, she went outside.

The village itself was clustered together, like people crowding for warmth. The streets were set in winding, uneven rows to avoid creating a terrible wind tunnel effect. The only things that existed outside of the village were several animal farmers and the monastery, which was home to the Red Order initiates.

Astral slipped behind the restaurant, keeping an ear out for spies as she pulled the pen apart, wide enough to reveal the full message. To anyone reading, it would have seemed like an ordinary letter from a concerned guardian to his ward, warning her to be careful and stay close to her group. But Dezmond had devised a way to communicate with his children and grandchildren in secret a long time ago.

Her grandfather's scrawled signature appeared at the bottom of the letter. In official correspondences he'd sign: D. Daamon. Today, he'd signed Gramps, which was her code name for him.

Astral removed her mitten and glove to touch her bare finger to her grandfather's signature. A new message appeared from Lord Leon, the Council's leader and founding father.

She read:

ASTRAL DAAMON, ESTEEMED HUNTER OF THE COUNCIL.

Astral narrowed her eyes at the word "esteemed". It would be one of those dangerous missions where, if she was caught, she'd have to deny the Council's involvement. She read on.

YOUR MISSION SHOULD YOU CHOOSE TO ACCEPT,

She arched a brow. Why did they imply that she had a choice? She'd have to accept the mission or deal with a permanent blemish on her civil record, which had its own series of less-than-ideal repercussions.

She had to press the "Accept" button before she could retrieve the briefing. This frustrated her. She'd like to know what the mission was before she accepted it, but that's not how these things worked. They were orders, plain and simple.

Lord Leon's face appeared on the screen, replacing the letter. The video waited as she detached the dull nib of the pen and put it into her ear. She touched the screen, signalling that she was ready for the transmission.

"It has come to our attention that members of the Red Order are taking part in occult activities. At this time, we are not sure of the truthfulness of the allegations, nor are we certain of the depth of their involvement.

"I've chosen you for this task on account of your experience with this faction, and the similarities to the Clearwater incident. We trust that your father had relayed information regarding their activities during that time to you. Given that you have already thwarted their plans once at such a tender age – at great expense to yourself – we humbly ask that you carry on in your father's stead.

"If we are correct in our assumption, it is your duty to determine the source of the Order's occult power and retrieve it. If of human or demon origin, eliminate it."

He paused, lowering his voice as though talking to a friend. "Townships in the vicinity of the Eternal Dawn Monastery have reported a rise in missing persons." He paused again, giving her time to digest the information. He was right to assume that she knew what this meant. It was one reason she and her father had travelled to Clearwater in her early childhood. "You'll report to Master Mathers regarding the artifact or persons involved. You will report directly to me on all other matters when the opportunity presents itself."

Leon concluded in a worried tone, "Child, do be careful."

His video vanished from her feed, its data wiped. She closed her viewfinder, reverting it to its thin, cylindrical shape, and commanded, "Seth Wright," then put it to her ear.

"Yes?" came Seth's voice. She could hear a news feed in the background, though she couldn't make out the words. There were only a handful of places where communications like that were available. She hoped that she wasn't interrupting him at work.

"You know how you said that I'd be interested in the architecture in Mountain Crest?"

"Sure," his voice warmed up. A week ago, Seth had contacted her about running a mission in Red Order territory. He wanted to know what assets an agent would need to successfully infiltrate a monastery through indirect means. At the time, he had assumed that he was going to be assigned the mission and wanted to be prepared.

"I have to say that I'm not all that impressed. I'm feeling lied to," she teased. Speaking openly about the mission was impossible, not with all of the added surveillance monitoring systems in all of their devices. A covert external investigation of the Red Order's grounds was enough to destroy tenuous alliances, causing the Red Order to withdraw their services from the populous. As much as Astral may have loathed the Red Order as an organization, their Hunters were necessary in slowing the demon's advance.

"Then you're not looking hard enough," Seth returned. "Tell you what. I'll make it easy on you and send a few references to look for. Don't bother with pictures for your report. It's an Order proclaimed Sacred zone. There are specialized fields a few miles out from the monastery that will disable your tech. If you need to make any calls, it'll have to be done while in town. You're with Mathias's group, right?"

"No, Mathias went to the Highland Monastery. William's with him. I went with Mrs. Price's advanced class... for extra credit," she felt she should add.

"The two-hour nap and a day out of class had nothing to do with it," he joked. They both knew that Mathias had advised her to take this trip so that she could investigate the monasteries activities on his behalf. Despite his standing within the Red Order, he was aware of the potential for hidden occult sects within the organization of which he had no access. He could not be in two places at once and it was better to split up the experienced Hunters to survey as many Red Order sites as covertly as possible. Astral thought nothing of it at the time, thinking she was little more than a set of trained eyes all while Mrs. Price was handing out homework, oblivious to the real purpose of the outing.

"Thanks. By any chance, can I just use your report?"

"Not a chance." Seth chuckled and hung up.

Astral regarded the device. Its nib flashed, signalling that she had another message. She split it open and pulled up the viewfinder. Sketches and blueprints flashed across the screen. She didn't have much time to study them.

೫つ୧

Astral licked her food cube as she watched the decoy, dressed in her winter clothes, follow her classmates on the town tour. Maybe she could get her decoy to do the history report...

"Can't tempt you?" the restaurateur offered her a plate of fresh food. "It's the least we can do, since you're looking into this for us. The Order just shrugged it off." His tone took a dark turn. "Some people were sent off to the front for murdering the missing folks, you know. They can't all have been murdered, can they? That's just ridiculous."

She declined the meal with a wave of her hand. "It's a strange coincidence," she replied. Murder would have been the first thought on her mind, too, yet there were no investigations, and no papers filed to inform the Council of a shipment of prisoners to the front. Her father had trained her well on how to keep tabs on their enemy, learn their habits, and watch for signs. Watching human predators did not differ from stalking demons. "Let's get on with it then, my timetable is limited."

The man nodded and escorted her down to the restaurant's cellar, where he revealed an old passage, hidden behind an empty antique wine cabinet. "It'll take you close to the monastery," he told her, as though he had explored it himself. "My great-uncle told me we used it during war times to evacuate the villagers to safer ground..." The way his voice trailed off hinted at a troubling thought. "It hasn't been used in over seventy-five years. I don't know what condition you'll find it in."

"I'll manage," Astral told him. "If anything happens, you know nothing." With that, she vanished into the darkness.

೫つ୧

In the damp cellar passage, a few feet from the exit that would take her to the alternate path to the monastery, Astral reviewed her notes one last time. Confident of her next steps, she slipped her tech under a dusty tarp that covered a cluster of abandoned furniture. The passage had served as the restaurants storage. She counted her steps three times from the exit, making sure that she knew where it was.

The passage opened up to a large path along the cliffside that ran up in a steep slope toward the monastery above. Beyond the path were light clouds and fog turned yellow under the glow of the morning sun. Icy mountain tops pierced the veil, their massive bodies disappearing into the mist that hid the valley below. The village sat on the opposite side of the cliff, in line with the monastery's main entrance. Astral watched the clouds dance over some unseen barrier. She felt that she had seen something like this somewhere in the distant past. It was a peaceful sight to behold.

She shrugged off the hazy memory and journeyed up the path, keeping close to the cliffside. When the mountain path narrowed until there was just enough room for one person to carry on, she heard water making its bid for freedom. It wasn't long before she found the source of the sound.

Ahead, she saw water pouring out of the side of the carved foundations of an old building. With no other entrance to the monastery, she pushed on toward the source of the water. She focused on the destination, forcing the deadly drop to her left from her mind as cascading sheets of water plummeted with suicidal zeal toward the rocks below. She heard the calls from the distant past: "It's not much further. This way! Have faith and the Lord shall save you!"

The ghostly cries of frightened villagers whimpered in her ear just as a deep winter chill passed through her. This place carried memories with it and repeated them, almost as though it were trying to tattletale.

Sticking to the cliffside, Astral travelled further down the steep, narrow path, holding her breath to focus on her footing. Up ahead, a row of larger-than-life statues were carved into the mountainside. The statues were in various states of ruin, marked the entrance to the catacombs. The rusted iron gates were twisted, pried apart in an attack ages ago, and the large, open entryway spat out the torrent of rushing water.

Astral waited for her heart to stop pounding against her chest before entering the catacomb.

As she proceeded deep into the darkness, the cries of the distraught and suffering inside carried across the water. She followed the current upstream as far as she could until the path split into a crossroads. Her options were to travel left or right in complete darkness, or to continue down the lit path straight ahead. The flickering of the torchlight felt out of place for a place that appeared as a story passed on through the generations. It was foolish to think someone was expecting her, since she'd had no plans to invade a Red Order monastery until arriving that morning.

Compelled by a distant memory, she followed the path ahead of her. Her fingers glided over the cold stone walls, bringing back ancient reminders of wandering in the darkness, singing to herself in a tongue she no longer recognized.

She caught herself humming and the jolt pulled her back from the memory. Was it hers, or did it belong to a spirit haunting these halls?

She searched for something real in the dim light. She couldn't trust her eyes, especially since firelight cast macabre shadows fueled by the imagination, desire, and expectation. She closed her eyes and search for a sound. This far in, her companions were the mournful cries of lost souls, the torrent of the guided refuse, and a slow but steady drip. The concentration needed to focus on the distant sound would force her to consciously push out all other details. Exactly what she needed to dispel a glamour.

The hypnotic pull of the tunnel melted away, taking with it the beacons, leaving her in complete darkness. The torches were an illusion, like wisps in the dark, leaving an unlucky traveler lost. She listened to the cries of despair resonate like a morbid choir.

These were not cries of physical harm. It was a deeper pain. They weren't calling out for help. They had long since stopped seeking comfort in the calls of their fellow inmates. She picked out the sounds of quick whispers, as though speaking to someone, followed by bursts of rage or anguish. Denial of their imprisonment wasn't possible in these bleak catacombs.

She reviewed the blueprints Seth had sent her in her mind, searching for some point of reference to help guide her. How far off course had she gone? Would she be able to find her way back? The sewer system within the catacombs were simple in design. All paths led to one exit, and everything was slanted to push the excretion out from the bowels of the monastery.

She realized that even if she freed these people from their despair, they would be forever altered, wondering if their new reality was some cruel illusion that their frail minds had conjured up to cope.

"This way." An airy whisper brushed against her ear. Without thinking, she stepped forward. A sudden force of willpower stopped her from carrying on. Her eyes narrowed in the darkness. "All this is for you," the whisper cooed, fading into the direction it had wanted her to travel.

"Astral?" the voice was much more real this time.

"Father?" She knew better than to believe it, but indulged the illusion. She couldn't see him, though she could feel his presence, could hear his heavy boots thud against the stone beneath his feet as he moved toward her. They were his footsteps, but something was off about the combination of sounds, such as the subtle scraping his feet made every time he lifted them.

"You shouldn't be here," he sounded so sincere, so worried. She nodded her approval at how real the illusion had become.

"I need to free them," she told him. "They don't deserve this."

He was silent. She could hear him breathing; it got heavier as he thought. He sighed. "It's complicated," he said at last. "You should leave."

She found it odd that the forces within this place would both lure her and urge her to leave. Something wasn't right. It was possible that the lure was designed to ensnare victims, but to avoid being found out, the Order's sorcerers had established a ward, intended to deter their enemies.

She wondered what would happen if she pressed on, taking a step forward to try her luck. Would the incantations fight one another? Would the entity posing as her father attack? Or would the dungeon swallow her whole? It all depended on which spell was more powerful.

"You don't understand what's going on," the man told her, his voice harsh and reprimanding, much in the same way he used to say, "Why can't you just get along with the other children?"

She wondered what lay beyond the magical barrier. Would this illusion tell her? It would no doubt bend the truth. "How many are there?" she demanded.

He considered his answer. "Too many to save."

"What's beyond here?" she asked.

She heard the ruffling of his clothes, as though he had gestured down the path. "Darkness; a void in time and space. No one who has entered has ever returned."

"You're here," she said.

"I never went in."

She gleaned a hidden meaning behind his words. Were the villagers being used to fetch something that could not be retrieved by mortal hands? Were their bodies in this world while their minds unravelled in the next? It was a frightening thought. "What are the prisoners being used for?" she blurted.

"I would have preferred to think of them as human batteries," he said, "charging some devious spell." Whatever the Red Order was using their captives for was far worse than perpetual anguish, especially if anguish itself was the fuel needed to activate the spell. It sounded like Hell. What was worse than Hell?

She pressed on, ignoring the illusion's warning.

The darkness became more tangible the deeper she went into the catacombs. The path she walked seemed to carry on into eternity, and she felt unseen eyes watching her as she passed by. She avoided touching the wall. She could feel it breathing, its living warmth pulsing next to her.

Astral could deny her fear to herself, but she felt that the darkness already knew how afraid she had grown. Why did it not swallow her whole? Why torture her so? She could reach out and touch the wall, feel its cold surface and dispel the illusion that her mind had conjured up. But there was the possibility that all of her senses were telling the truth.

Step by step, she felt the solid ground under her boots, the sound unchanging.

One step too far and her world went from pure darkness to brilliant white, momentarily blinding her. She had entered a wide open space, in a reality that didn't fit the world that she had come from. The room was white – not a sterile white as seen in hospitals, but the pure and brilliant white that one associated with heavenly bodies – and the ceiling so high that mist had formed halfway up. As the fog rippled, she glimpsed stars and the void beyond.

The barriers shaping the walls were easily one hundred feet apart; though she had just entered the room, she stood in the middle of it. This wasn't a room, she realized. She had stepped into a rift, into a place between realms.

There were people in the room with her, all broken. Some of them still had solid forms, bearing cracks in their skin from which light escaped. Others were shapeless, featureless entities, barely conscious of their new companion. There were a few hundred, all in varying stages of transformation, moving about the space without purpose or direction.

Astral's own physical form was altered. In this world, she was a being of darkness that shone with the same ferocity as the light in the room. It welcomed her, as though acknowledging the return of a long-time friend.

She inspected herself, arms and legs still attached; all ten digits, check. She didn't feel any different. Her motives were still the same. She had a mission to complete, people to save, and a spell to disrupt.

She heard chanting. It wasn't coming from this room, which existed in its own reality. It was coming from somewhere beyond the walls. When she looked around to find its source, she instead saw that a pedestal had appeared before her with a thick, ratty old book sitting atop, almost like a pet greeting its master.

She reached for the book, stroking its surface. A glyph burned into the cover underneath her fingers and the book snapped open, the pages turning with savage ferocity as it searched for the right one. She could not read its text.

The people in the room had stopped their aimless wandering. For the first time in a very long time, they were coherent. With their lucidity came fear and confusion.

From beyond the walls, there was shouting in a language that seemed familiar, yet still so foreign. Astral realized that the window of opportunity was narrow. The Order's sorcerers would regroup and try again, whatever they were doing.

She shouted at the damaged souls. "Get out! Run! You're free!" Run they did, vanishing into the light as they conjured their own exits, formed no doubt by their own personal realities. It didn't matter if they made it to the real world, as long as they were no longer trapped in this fading existence.

The pure energy of the rift changed. Pieces of the pristine white barriers broke apart, revealing the pulsating flesh beneath, and blood oozed out, covering the floors in vile sludge as it picked its way toward the Demon Hunter.

The room groaned, allowing thirteen shadow figures into this new reality. They moved toward her like beasts pretending to be men but halted after a few steps, unable to breach the wide untainted area that Astral was in.

Weaponless, perhaps, but a Hunter had to take down the enemy using anything available to her; that included the beast itself.

In unison, the shadows raised their left hands. Dark energy shot from their fingers like lightning, striking at the protective seal around Astral. The ground began to rot away. The book lay open in Astral's hands, sketched an illustration onto its pages: a young heroine surrounded by demons, but protected by a dome of light as she held the book to her chest.

When Astral pulled the book to her chest, she felt something primal surge through her. It was as though all the knowledge in its contents flooded her mind. This was more than just a collection of stories. It was someone's experiences. It was someone's reality.

In that moment, she was no longer the Council's esteemed Hunter. She was that someone, a woman from so many millennia ago, facing down a familiar foe. She extended her hand, willing the dome to shrink to her touch, and held it for a second, staring down the shadowy figure directly ahead of her.

Then, she willed the seal to expand, tearing at the corruption surrounding her and smashing the dark figures into their hellish reality. Human and demon arms formed from the fleshy walls and tore at the shadow men who cried out in agony.

The ground beneath Astral gave way. In one last act of self-preservation, her possessed body grabbed onto the ledge before releasing her from its spell.

The pit below was filled with bodies in various states of decomposition, and the ground onto which she held hovered in the air. She knew that the magic suspending that piece in place would soon fade as the rest of this dimension's magic completed its transition into another alternate realm.

Something swooped down from above, landing on the remains of the floating floor. Glancing up, she saw a moving mass of crimson red cloth as a figure reached down to pull her up, just enough so that she could do the rest of the job herself. The figure yanked the heavy book from her hand with ease, using her situation against her. Before she could get a look at his face, he turned away and leaped into the pit.

Whoever it was, he had seen her. She'd save the disaster of covering up her mission for the politicians.

Right now, she had one last thing to do: seal the rift before it unleashed God knew what kind of monstrosities upon the village.

This whole ordeal was reminiscent of the Clearwater incident from her childhood: demons had swarmed the town, killing many of its residents. It was the day that she had lost her father to the Red Order's Crimson Knights and won her reputation as a natural-born Demon Hunter.

The tragic event occurred during an annual local celebration. The Red Order altered reality to break an ancient seal and unleash a powerful weapon upon the world. Perhaps they hoped to fight the emerging demon hoards with another demon they thought to control. Astral didn't know for sure what they were after, but she was acutely aware of the devastation and a new brand of problems that came with their ritual.

If she wanted to save the village of Mountain Crest from the same fate, she would have to dive deeper into the rift before the breach became large enough to allow the monsters to escape. At that moment, the rest of the floor crumbled away, forcing her into the dark reality below.

Her landing was wet. The pooled sludge from the piles of decomposing bodies oozed around her. She wanted to gag, but feared that if she did, she wouldn't stop. The ground was uneven beneath her feet, hidden in the murky fluid. Several mounds of bodies had been formed over time, six in her immediate vicinity, easily fifty more in the area beyond, from what she could see. She peered upward, seeing a pinprick of light above in this otherwise dark world.

Throaty chanting emanated from the sky like the voice of the gods. It droned on in a consistent, dominating rhythm. It had a certain draw to it, as though calling to its denizens.

Astral heard the crunching of bones and the noisy slurping of hungry predators as they feasted on the remains somewhere in the distance. She crouched down low, hoping to avoid being spotted. A chorus of piercing shrieks rang out; the creatures turned on one another, clawing and hissing, as they tried to rob partially chewed morsels from each other's mouths.

She peered around the mound to get a look at the threat. They were small and child-like with the bloated, round bellies of those who are starving. Some had pointed ears, while others had none. Their soulless black eyes were wide as saucers, and their mouths giant, splitting their faces from ear to ear, and filled with rows of tiny, jagged teeth. If she survived this ordeal, she would have to research these goblin-like creatures in Dezmond's library.

A thunderous explosion struck the goblins, scattering their small bodies around the mound. Those who survived fled.

"You there!" a woman called as she emerged from behind a mound of her own. She shot two more rounds from her shotgun into the packs of feeding goblins who had ignored her previous deadly warning. The woman had a muscular frame, dark skin, and dark, matted hair. She wore demon hides as clothing and had fashioned some of it into primitive armour. Astral stood tall, hiding her fear. "Oh, my!" the woman gasped. Flickers of light appeared in the cracks across her body. She was doing everything that she could to keep herself together. "You're... Are you?" she struggled to find the words to speak.

"I am self-aware," Astral told the woman. "Am I in the demon world?"

"More like a nightmare world," the woman sneered. "Before you ask, I don't know how long I've been here. We're here because of that." She gestured to the pinprick of light in the sky. Astral nodded. "The demons are migrating toward it. If that rift goes to our world, then I'll be damned if I'm letting any of these monsters get through."

Other beings worked their way over the field of the dead, fighting off creatures of all kinds. Most of the fighters were human, with bright fissure scars, much like the spirits from the previous reality. Some had lost limbs or portions of their bodies, and hides had been used to mask the light that attempted to escape from their broken bodies. They reminded Astral of broken vases that had been glued back together

The humans worked in units, moving like a well-oiled machine, though not without its flaws. They had to use a great deal of energy to take down a larger demons who were migrating toward the rift. Hungry goblin packs seemed content to follow the small army of human souls, spying potential meals and helping to take down bigger prey.

"I'm here to stop them from carrying out their plan," Astral told the woman.

"You'll fight?" she asked. Astral nodded. The woman handed her a makeshift sword carved out of a long, thick demon bone. Astral tested it against the nearest mound, slicing clean through the pile of the dead with little effort. The weapon wouldn't last long, but it might do well enough to get her out of this pit. "And you prefer the gun?" Astral smirked.

"Don't have to get up close and personal that way," the woman offered as an explanation. "We're headed that way," she nodded in one direction. "If we seal the gate, we won't be able to get back..." the fissures in her dark skin cracked a little more, "but we'll be able to save our families."

The survivors closed the remaining distance between themselves and Astral, suspicion clear in their haunted expressions.

"Shield bearers!" the woman commanded and gestured to Astral. Two damaged souls took their place next to her, each holding a tall shield made of a combination of scales, hide, and sharp fangs.

Astral turned to resume her mission, but the woman grabbed her arm. A moment passed between them as she stared into the eternity that was Astral's soul. She nodded to her as though understanding the reality of their plight.

"Don't risk our families to bring us back," the woman told her. "We want to have a place to go back to. Out there," she gestured to the widening pinprick in the sky. "You fight for us. In here, we'll fight for them." The woman and her men were among those reported missing in from the township of Mountain Crest. In this Hell, they had found their purpose and reforged their resolve to protect their families by fighting demons from within the rifts. Astral nodded, she wouldn't try to find a way to bring these lost souls home, as per their request.

Shield bearers in tow, Astral took off in the direction the woman had pointed out, fighting off anything that got in her way.

The closer she got to the source of the spell, the louder the chanting grew. The words echoed through her mind, pounding the rhythm into her heart. It became difficult to breathe. She had crossed a invisible threshold and entered into a space that was saturated with magic. The energy of the area would only intensify as she neared the source. Rotted corpses strewn the area with the mounds set up as morbid sentry posts surrounding the magically charged area.

In the center of the death site was a large man in ebony plated armor basking in the beam of light that fell from the rift above. He gazed up at it in wonder and awe. At first glance, he looked human. He had a handsome face and square jaw with pearly white teeth; the features suited to a hero.

But when his attention fell on Astral, his inhumanity was clear. His eyes were large and black, much like those of the goblins, his matted dreadlocked hair were masses of writhing centipedes, and his face bore more hog-like features than human. It was difficult to conceive how such a humanoid demon could exist naturally within a demonic rift. She approached, watching as his hand tightened its grip over his whip.

"A new trophy," his voice was unlike anything she had ever heard. Cold and precise, like dripping water into a deep well. The jagged barbs that made up his weapon snapped past her face, but she was quick to dodge the lash, remaining on course. She had seen it coming and denied the demon his taunt.

His charming smile faded. "No demon or human has ever evaded one of my attacks!" With another crack of his whip, he struck at the shield bearers, destroying their defences. She stopped and motioned for her defenders to leave. They had escorted her to the intended destination. There was no point in keeping them around for a fight that would get them killed. This man was a demon champion, whose skills were forged by sheer will power and survival. He was not a threat to take lightly. But neither was she.

She didn't give them the opportunity to argue, resuming her course toward the demonic fighter. "I am not a demon," she told him, "and neither are these souls. But then again, you knew that, didn't you?"

His lips twisted into a cruel smirk. He extended his free hand, reaching toward the retreating spirits, uttering words that shook the earth on which they ran, stealing their breath and what remained of their life force, leaving nothing behind.

Satisfied, he lifted his hand to the sky and shouted words that no human tongue could pronounce. The beam of light grew wider, engulfing the man completely. The whole time, he never took his gaze off Astral, but his psychic grasp could not grab onto fragments of her soul.

Intrigue played across his features. At the crack of his whip, Astral pulled her demon blade to her body. The whips' tongue wrapped around her neck and weapon, intending to break her as he had many others before her. The barbs bit into her arm and neck but gave her just enough room to breathe.

"What kind of demon are you?" he demanded, as though reprimanding his subordinate.

Astral twisted her blade to cut into the living whip. allowing the barbs to tear into the skin. With a flick of her wrist the demon sword severed the whip's hold. She pointed the sword to the demon and uttered the words that rang in her mind.

There was power in those words, especially when released into existence. They stung the demon and the wounded whip slithered into

Astral's hand as though it now belonged to her.

"Magic!" the demon spat as though the words left a foul taste in his mouth. He retreated a few steps, moving out of the light, as she stepped forward and into it. She stared down at the demon man as the weapon leaped out toward its previous owner, twisting around his body. It squeezed and tore into him, transforming its barbs into sharp, living tendrils that hungered for more demon blood, until he and his weapon lay dead at her feet.

Astral stared up into the light. Human souls were used to open the gate. What could she use to seal it? Looking back into the demon world, she saw legions of demons marching toward the rift, still some distance away.

She racked her memory for a solution. She had heard tales of the First; the deity worshipped by men like her grandfather, who had sealed away the demon lords and their armies into their own personal hells. But these legends told nothing of how they were sealed.

Could she close the gate from in here? Or could it only be done from her world? Either way, she didn't want to stay in this abyss.

As though that thought was all it took, the light embraced her, and the world around her faded.

She was human again. It was peculiar how trapped she suddenly felt in her own body, so much so that she found it difficult to breathe. She felt a hand on her back, stroking it as she struggled for air. Her father's voice told her, "Slow, deep breaths."

She faked struggling a little longer than she needed to get acquainted with her surroundings. She was in a stone chamber with torches along the wall. The Red Order occultists were dead, their blood pooling to the drain in the center of a pit. She and the man in the ruined red robes were in the pit which was covered in a multitude of glyphs and elaborate magic circles. Half of a magic circle had been drawn in blood, incomplete in its symbols. From what she could tell she was standing over the bloodied drain at the center of the ruined ritual. She saw a grey clawed hand to her left, dripping with blood. This creature next to her – did he kill the Red Order sorcerers?

"You need to head into town," he told her, "and bind the gate to a pure soul."

"Why are you helping me?" she asked, too afraid to look the beast in the eyes.

He slid the heavy tome that she had seen in the alternate reality onto her lap. "He will come for you," he said, pulling her to her feet. All the while he remained behind her, out of sight. He didn't want to be seen. She didn't want to know that he was real.

"Who?" she asked.

"Never mind that. You need to go!"

A demon's clawed hand was reaching out from the summoning circle in front of her, attempting to pull itself through.

"I'll stay to finish the binding on this end and to make sure nothing gets through," he told her. "I can't be in two places at once!"

Tome in hand, she ran into the darkness of the catacombs.

ᏝᏯᏨ

"I see," the young waitress replied while removing her eccentric winter disguise.

Astral found herself at odds with what needed to be done. On the one hand, the knowledge of the seal would be a burden to anyone she told. That same knowledge could also be turned into a devastating weapon if she told the wrong person. She didn't have enough time to report to the Council and wait for their decision. She didn't need a Council puppet, she needed someone with the grit and willpower to do what was right. Someone with a soul to sacrifice.

So, she did the only thing that she thought sensible for the time. She told the young woman who had sent her tearful plea to Mathias some months ago. Her tears were for her sister, her best friend's family, for her neighbour, and for the men and women convicted of murders they did not commit. Her tears were for the innocent lives lost.

"So they're stuck there?" she asked, her voice shaking.

Astral shrugged. "They were sent there. I think once I'm strong enough, I can get them back, but as things stand..."

"And if the gate opens..." She looked out the restaurant's window to the monastery. "I'll do it."

"I don't think you'll ever be able to leave this town," Astral told her. "It might also pass down to your children. It's a huge responsibility, some might say a curse even."

"But as long as I'm alive, that seal will stay shut," the waitress confirmed.

"It's more complicated than that, but yes."

She frowned. "Isn't that like witchcraft or something?"

"No ju-ju, no chanting, no potions. It's no different from promising to take care of your parents when they get old," Astral said. "You know what's there, and you know what will happen if you fail. It's a heavy burden. By virtue of agreeing, the binding is complete."

"I'll do it," the waitress said.

The simple act of volunteering for the role, knowing what was at stake, was enough to do the job. Astral would have liked fireworks to prove that the magic had taken hold, but in this world that wasn't how magic worked at all.

It was getting close to her departure time. Astral rejoined her classmates at the shops, hoping that her absence had gone unnoticed and that her decoy had performed as expected. Mrs. Price approached her as she admired a handmade scarf.

"Are you all right dear?" the teacher asked. "That initiate had no right to treat you like that."

Astral smiled beneath her scarf and shrugged off the event she knew nothing about. "I spoke with his instructor, if that helps at all," Mrs. Price continued. "But it got me to thinking. You're not much different from that boy." Astral returned her crystalline gaze to the scarf, hoping to avoid a subconscious rolling of her eyes. "You might treat everyone the same, but you place yourself at an elevated position, superior to the rest. The world will work very hard to prove your arrogance."

She listened, taking in each word. She was insulted but recognized the truth in the words. Would it change her behaviour? Maybe…

"You are very good at what you do. No one can dispute your greatness in that respect. Your comment this morning suggests that you might do even greater things that don't involve killing monsters for a living. But for now, I want you to think on what a true hero is. I hope that you do so much better than our past heroes… I hope that you become so much more. Do you know what I'm saying?"

Astral hadn't a clue where her instructor was going with this, but nodded anyway.

"Just remember that it wouldn't take much for you to be that boy you met at the monastery today. One step in the wrong direction can take years to get you back on track."

Astral frowned. Mrs. Price was referencing the Red Order initiate, but she felt an odd chill run up her spine. It wouldn't take much for Astral to become the monster she faced in the hell dimension, either.

"Anyway, enough with this old lady's lecture!" Mrs. Price smiled at her student before leaving to shepherd her class toward the shuttle that would take them back to the Academy.

Astral felt the book tucked under her coats call to the world at large. "What is a hero?" she asked herself, her thoughts hazed by the magic that guarded the tome.

STORY V
SHADOW PREY
PART I

SHADOW PREY: PART I

Early morning light filtered through the tall library windows. The word "library" was an archaic description of the room; physical books had long since been abandoned by society in favour of their much lighter digital counterparts. Instead of row upon row of shelves and books, there were rows of thin screens on white bases into which students could plug their tablets and pull the information that they wanted for future reference. As a result, this room, despite early eighteenth century décor, was more like a study hall.

Two rows of tables lined the right side of the room, closest to the windows, followed by a gap that separated the dedicated study space from the librarian's desk, which was placed on top of rich green carpeting. The rest of the library flooring was a complex network of light and dark hardwood patterns stretching far back to the decorative glass divide where the pupils could access information databanks in private.

A small green lamp was still glowing, despite the dawn. The student it served had long since fallen asleep. Hidden beneath a mass of dishevelled black hair was an old tome. The cursive script and illustrations inside suggested that its origins dated long before the printing press had revolutionized the book industry.

The light above the library's main doors flashed green before permitting a man in his early thirties to enter. Mathias Mathers was of average height, only a few inches above six feet, with the healthy complexion of a man who liked to spend his time outdoors.

He spotted the sleeping girl. It had been a long night worrying over her safety and the general outcome of her mission. He had been sixteen before he was assigned his first independent mission without the help of his Master, but his apprentice had been functioning without supervision for far longer. In the few years that she'd had with her father, he had trained her into a skilled Hunter.

He pulled at his coat in a vain attempt to straighten it further. The styles permitted to a Master of the Order lent themselves to the old Victorian fashions, almost as a tribute to their unchanging traditions and beliefs. Master Mathers liked the simplicity of his wardrobe. The only thing he had to concern himself with was the touch of red required to represent his allegiance and training. The shirt that peeked out from his sleeves and high collar was the shade of crimson worn by all members of the Order.

His steps echoed with purpose as he made his way to the sleeping figure. When he reached her, he stopped to watch for a moment.

The fifteen-year-old girl had come back at some godless hour that very morning from a successful retrieval mission. Mathias had allowed her the opportunity to inspect the curious artifact after reporting to him. She asked for very little. He saw no harm in satisfying her curiosity, at least for the night.

Part of him believed that she had her reasons for being curious. He'd always suspected that she had residual knowledge from a previous incarnation, and he didn't want to impede her from her interests at the risk of having her filter out crucial information.

He reminded himself that she was a teenage girl. As his unruly apprentice, he couldn't afford insubordination without risking her walking all over him.

"Daamon," he barked.

"Five more minutes," Astral mumbled.

His own Master would have pulled the chair out from under him for such casual disregard of his authority. "You have another mission," he snapped.

"Ten more minutes then," she murmured and repositioned herself so that the morning light no longer washed over her face.

He stared down at her, fearful of the backlash of her hidden abilities. It was in this lazy state, when she was least herself, that he worried that her powers might roam. In her normal state, she was in control but otherwise oblivious to her true potential.

"Demons have invaded the compound," he tried to sound urgent.

She mumbled something that he didn't quite understand, but she didn't rouse, all sense of urgency going over her head.

"Don't do the chair thing!" she shouted as though waking up from a vivid dream. She looked around, disorientated and confused. Her crystalline stare narrowed and focused on her Master. Sometimes when she looked at him, he could sense a trace of resentment. Did she blame him for the murder of her father? Or was it something else?

"There is no mission, is there?" she finally asked.

He cocked his head, wondering how coherent her thinking was.

"Actually, there is. Preparations for transport are being finalized. You'll be leaving as soon as they're ready."

She regarded him with her sleepy stare as her mind worked to put the pieces together. She looked down at herself, still dressed in her black battle gear. Classes were due to start in two hours. Her regular attendance was expected, mission or not. She had time to make herself presentable before her dorm mates woke, flooding the facilities.

Astral shut the book with a loud thud and handed it over to her Master. "I would have liked more time to study it," she told him, rising from her seat.

At her full height, she was a foot shorter than Mathias, but despite her shorter stature she carried herself with an air of authority. He suspected that it wouldn't be long before she'd be giving him orders to carry out.

She said nothing else and walked out, leaving him no time to dismiss her.

Mathias regarded the tome in his hands. Engraved in its deep red cover was a familiar circular glyph.

₧)₡

Half asleep, Astral mused over last night's findings while changing into her school uniform. The book was written in an old tongue and likely translated a few times from the original text. Her grandfather would be the best person to interpret the bulk of the writing. What she found interesting were the illuminations.

She checked her battle gear for general wear and tear before hanging it up, then pulled her long white coat over her short pleated skirt and silky blouse, fastening its twin rows of buttons from her waist to her neck. She pinned a silver cross broach to the collar of her shirt, which marked her as an apprentice.

The lights dimmed in the changing room. Astral ignored it. The surge fled as quickly as it had come, restoring full light to the area as students began to trickle in.

Astral nodded to passersby and set off to start her day.

₧)₡

The teacher's voice droned on about the historical data that led to the collapse of the old world. In this lesson, they were talking about the rise of war machines, bulky robotic vehicles that were piloted by two or three men at a time.

The noise fell away as Astral occupied her time by staring outside. It was a beautiful spring morning that had brought with it unseasonal warmth. The novice training classes were enjoying a lesson outdoors.

She watched their lazy movements, boys and girls flexing and stretching to show off their bodies, and small clusters of students talking through the session, causing them to lag in their instructor's commands. Of the group, she could pick out the few who were very much aware of the threat beyond the compound walls. The children whose families lived in towns on the surface were always keen to learn survival skills.

Sudden giggling drew her attention away from the trainees and back to the class.

"Had your fill?" the teacher asked again, smirking as she gestured with a nod toward the trainees that Astral had been observing.

Astral regarded the students again and sighed. "That depends on the information that you want."

A few girls at the back snickered. Teasing would no doubt follow about how clueless she was. Astral understood the insinuation. She ignored it. An idea that never crossed their primitive, hormone-addled minds.

"Students A2, C3, and E5 won't ever have to set foot on the front lines and they know it," Astral commented. "B4, C1, C5, D2 and D4 have potential. E2, E3, and E4 will attempt to take command of their unit, likely ending in total annihilation." To the people who didn't know her very well this statement appeared rude, even arrogant. Who was she to assume the fate of the students in training? Those who were familiar with her growing reputation as a Hunter suspected that there may be some truth in her words.

Her peers had piled up against the window to get a glimpse of what she was talking about. With the students distracted, Astral redirected her attention onto the teacher, holding her in a mental grip. The teacher gasped as the breath lodged itself in the back of her throat, as her mind was pulled back and forth through time, revealing her secrets. Astral probed the teacher's soul. Was she a good person? Did she have an agenda? Astral found nothing and released the poor, simple woman from her hold. Seconds had passed between them, but Astral had seen her wasted life, ruled by the whims of another.

The teacher opened her mouth to scold the student, but nothing came out.

The girls at the window burst out in excited screams. "It's him! Oh my god, he's so—"

Astral glanced outside, indifferent to the fuss of her classmates. Seth crossed the courtyard to the main offices. A former instructor had approached him, wanting him to show off a few moves to inspire the students in training.

As though sensing that he was being watched, he glanced up at the classroom. His icy stare matched Astral's in intensity. They shared a silent conversation.

Seth was four years older than Astral. He had graduated a year ago and chose to spend his remaining year within the compound to help train advanced classes. These days he was running missions and training his own team for the Council. He had been one of the first people to greet her when she had arrived with the new group of initiates and had singled her out for immediate induction into the apprentice program.

While he would not become her Master, she liked to think they had learned a great deal from one another. Seth's reputation as a Hunter started in his early teens and only grew with each mission he undertook. In a few years, Astral knew that his story would be legendary.

Seth was over six feet tall, having grown a few more inches since she had seen him last, towering over the novices who stared up at him in awe. He kept his dark hair tied back with a white ribbon and his features were cold, though there was no mistaking that he was male. He had an otherworldly look to him, almost as though he had been sculpted using the finest materials.

He was wearing a long leather officer's coat that cut off at the ankles, though in the spring warmth, he had forsaken formal protocols and left it unfastened, revealing his battle gear beneath it. He was here on a mission.

Gossip was called to a stop as the teacher attempted to get her class back on track, but she was interrupted when a chime rang from her desk and a message appeared on the wooden surface. The red heading flashed with urgency.

The teacher read through the message then regarded the apprentice that it concerned as though this were a great inconvenience. "Lady Daamon, the Council requires your presence," she announced.

The classroom filled with whispers, some even jumping to the correct conclusions.

"You suppose Seth is here to escort her?" one student guessed.

"Oh, I hope not," another whined. "*I* want to get private lessons!"

The teacher allowed the class a moment before adding, "You'll report to Master Mathers for details." Astral rose from her seat. "I'll expect your assignment handed in by the next class," the teacher stated, hoping to maintain some level of authority.

Astral regarded her. For the short time that Astral held the teacher's gaze she felt time slow. "I might be away for some time. You will have to send details of the documentation that you require from me, along with the deadlines," she replied.

The teacher could only stare after the apprentice long after she had left the classroom. She always felt so unsettled around that girl.

ഇൗയ

Astral slowed her pace as she made her way down the hall of the administration wing to Mathias's office. She didn't want to appear eager for the dangerous work that lay ahead. The fact that Seth was here made her extra cautious of her actions.

Mathias's rebellious son, William, had always gone to great lengths to tease Seth about the rumours regarding the pair. Astral suspected that it had been William who started a fair few of them, for entertainment value, but Seth never acknowledged his antics.

Over the past two years, she had observed William's secret rivalry with Seth grow. William had talent as a Hunter but seemed frustrated to find himself living in Seth's shadow.

The hall lights dimmed as she got closer to her destination. The air became hard to breathe. It reminded her of the place where she had found the tome. It seemed to harken back to a distant memory of being trapped in absolute darkness. The memory pulled at her soul, calling her into it.

But the sounds of two men arguing kept her from lingering in hazy recollection too long. She came to a halt outside of Mathias's office, listening to him go head-to-head with Seth.

Their arguments had become more frequent over the past year. She did not understand what had spurred their sudden dislike for one another, but the years of working together wasn't helping them find common ground.

"You're wasting her talents on thievery," Seth sneered, "and now you're wasting them on a delivery job."

"Last I checked, Wright, I am her Master and she will perform the duties I require of her," Mathias replied in the same tone.

"You mean the duties that you would rather not do yourself."

"An apprentice does as commanded." He wished that were true in Astral's case. "Oh, for Heaven's sake, get in here Daamon!"

"Are you sure?" Astral called from the hall. "I don't really want to be involved in this." She would have preferred just to listen in.

"Get in here," Seth snapped.

Astral entered the office, hands behind her back.

Seth closed the door behind her to prevent anyone else from eavesdropping. "Did you have any trouble with the Red Order's security?" he asked.

"Some," she replied with a shrug. "It wasn't anything that I couldn't handle." Concern flashed across his cold features. During the planning phase of the mission, he didn't think she would get assigned to the mission. She had kept her source a secret, even from Mathias. Mathias was under constant scrutiny of the Red Order and only cooperated with the Council covertly or when ordered. Seth worked for the Council, and it was in the Council's best interest not to reveal just how much they new about their political rival. It made dealing with both Seth and Mathias at the same time challenging.

Seth had been her informant for blueprints of the monastery and had warned her about the anti-tech shielding. He had gone to great lengths to make sure she had everything that she needed for a safe retrieval of the ancient manuscript. Though at the time of her assignment, she was meant to determine the source of the occult activity surrounding Mountain Crest and destroy it. A handover was requested only after learning she had stolen a source of power from the Red Order.

"The rumours are true then," he pressed.

"That depends on the rumour," Astral dodged the question. "I'm not sure the defences I encountered were planned. If you know of a way to trigger a gate to Hell when I steal your morning coffee, I'm all ears. From what little I could glean of the text and illuminations, I think the book is cursed."

Seth cast her a doubtful look. "You buy into superstitions too easily."

"And there's a whole side of this world that you ignore," she retorted. "You dismiss tall tales and mythology only because of how the story is told. Just think about how your adventures will be told hundreds of years from now."

"You assume that his story will survive that long," Mathias cut in. "Sit and we'll get down to business."

Astral took her seat in front of her Master's desk as she had done countless times before.

"Lord Leon himself has called you to the capital to meet with him. I don't know what it's regarding, but I know that you will be away for a week. Daamon, you will stay with your grandfather. Wright, they have arranged accommodations for you."

Seth knew that he hadn't been called from his work only to receive an invitation through Mathias. He regarded Astral in silence. It wasn't a coincidence that he was leaving with her. Though he didn't have all the information, he understood that if the mission involved both of them, it was likely classified as dangerous, or perhaps even suicidal.

Mathias continued. "Daamon, you are required to leave as you are. No battle gear, no weapons."

All emotion melted away from Seth's face. He was impossible to read in this state, and he would maintain it throughout the brief and for some time afterwards as he worked out how to best handle the mission ahead.

Astral, on the other hand, was not so composed. "You've got to be kidding me!" Astral shouted. In a world where she'd have to stifle her thoughts and shape her identity based on other people's wants, Mathias allowed her the rare privilege of expressing herself freely in his presence. He felt it was a fair trade given how often the world jeopardized her life for their continued safety.

"Officially, you are only visiting with your grandfather. It would be strange if you arrived at the city armed. Seth will serve as your escort. It's time that you learned to trust someone with your life. Let him do his job and everything will work out. You'll see." But there was doubt in her Master's eyes.

"You can trust me to take you to the capital," Seth said, the hint of a question lingering in his voice.

"That's not the point."

"Is there a reason for concern?" Mathias asked.

"I'm to deliver the tome, isn't that right? As much as I'd like to assume that the Order isn't even aware that it's missing, it has a certain draw to it."

She sat back in her chair, thinking back to the previous night. "I could have found the book without the schematics. At one point I was working blind, but its... pull guided me toward it."

Mathias's gaze snapped to Seth, searching for an indication that he could feel the power of the book himself. But, while Seth had no doubts in what Astral was saying, he didn't feel the same way.

"You'll be travelling by day which should be an advantage," Mathias assured his apprentice. "You should arrive at the capital by sunset; after which, the shields will do the rest."

"I don't have a choice, do I," she sighed.

"I'll arrange decoys just in case the Red Order knows of the theft," Seth told her. "We will also switch vehicles several times throughout the day. Your safety is my top priority." He turned to Mathias. "I trust that I'll be escorting her back?"

"I believe that's the intention," the Master replied.

"And the tome?" Astral pressed. Her intuition told her that Seth's plan would only confuse humans, and though they would travel to the capital city during the day, reducing the likelihood of a demon attack, it was not impossible. Both men were certain that they had covered their bases. Astral remained unconvinced.

Mathias pushed a package on his desk toward her. "Don't open it and treat it with care."

When she touched the box, she couldn't feel it resonate. She knew that the book was somewhere in this room, just not in this box. Mathias arched a brow, noting her confused expression. "Your senses aren't lying, Daamon. The book is not in this package. You are dismissed."

She took the box and left the room. She could only speculate what Mathias had in mind at this point.

Mathias nodded to Seth, dismissing him too.

Seth followed his charge as she made her way through the school corridors, deep in her own thoughts. He realized something about this mission was troubling her. Perhaps there was something that he had overlooked.

The main doors of the Academy's administration office to the outside world opened, washing them both in light from outside. A black car with tinted windows was waiting for them in the driveway. Upon seeing them, the driver got out of the car and opened the door to the back seat.

Philip was bald, clean shaven, and solidly built. He had broad shoulders and was taller than Seth by two inches. Beneath his immaculately pressed suit was a toned, muscular frame.

Philip had always seemed a little off to Seth. Behind his reflective shades, Seth knew there were a pair of yellow cybernetic implants.

When researching into Philip's history, all Seth could find out was that he had been Dezmond's bodyguard for almost twenty years. Short of retrieving Astral every now and again, he was rarely seen away from Dezmond.

Philip nodded to Astral, who nodded her greeting in return as she climbed into the back seat and slid over. Seth followed, pausing at the door and offering a weak smile as he scrutinized the man.

"How are you today?" Seth asked. Not once had he ever heard the bodyguard speak.

This time was no different.

Seth climbed in next to Astral. "I don't think he likes me," he told her as Philip closed the door behind him.

"Philip doesn't like or dislike anyone," Astral replied. "He has his duties, and that's all. I'm sure you can relate on that front."

"You get along with him?"

"I know that I can trust him," she admitted.

The car pulled away from the Academy and soon they were outside of the protective barrier.

❧

The journey took them north where the snow was in no danger of melting. A thick overcast replaced the bright, blue skies, releasing a flurry of light snow.

Every hour they switched vehicles while under the cover of a tunnel, protecting them from ancient satellite feeds and sky drones.

Seth monitored the gaps in security camera footage where they were scheduled to make the switch. Timing was critical. The blackouts changed on a random schedule.

Astral leaned in as Seth explained the idea, showing her the video feed as seen by anyone watching it. Occasionally, she would glimpse a car or truck speeding by the camera. He refused to tell her how he had gained access to the footage or how he had discovered that there were gaps in the feeds that they could exploit.

She was silent for some time while watching the feeds. Seth could only guess at what she was thinking.

His tablet flashed, signalling that he had to decide on the switch. "Barrier 12," he told Philip, who nodded in acknowledgement. The car pulled to a stop next to an older, more popular model, which sat next to the number: a bright yellow, stencilled number twelve.

Philip switched cars with them, while the driver of the other vehicle took theirs. Once everyone had settled into the car, Philip in the front, Seth and Astral in the back, the journey continued.

The car was more cramped than Seth would have liked. He found his proximity to his charge uncomfortable.

"I thought for sure you would have been sent to the war front," Astral commented. Talking about either the mission or of a known want were her usual fail-safes. He had seen her use this tactic on other people with success.

The corners of Seth's lips curled into a sad smile. They had denied his enlistment. Under most circumstances, any able-bodied male had to register unless he had enough wealth to pay for his freedom. Since he was not of the latter class, he knew that he would have to go to the front lines of the war and face the demons head-on if he ever wanted to live his life.

As an invalid in the eyes of the military, his ability to earn gainful employment dropped. Until he served his time on the Killing Fields, he had no future, just stuck as an indentured servant to the Council and its people, unable to refuse his missions or transition into a different career.

Astral arched a brow. "Come on, it's not like they have any real standards. They send out thugs and the lower class without a second thought."

He sighed. "My father wants to run a few more tests; he's been my biggest obstacle. He's convinced the military to keep me from combat."

"It's because you were sick as a kid, right?" she asked.

He nodded. "I assume so. There's been no sign of that illness since I was nine. I think my father enjoys torturing me."

She thought for a moment. "Maybe you're being prepared for a different role. Have you considered that?" He regarded her, contemplating the possibility. She continued, "It's no secret that Lord Leon plans on choosing his successor from the Academy. Let's face it, the classes aren't exactly normal. We have to learn our maths and sciences and so on, but combat training, technological studies, politics, etiquette—"

"We know which classes you've skipped." Seth laughed. The administration encouraged girls of certain social standing to learn homemaking skills such as cooking and cleaning because they wouldn't be able to fetch a wealthy match and therefore could never afford to hire maids or butlers. Etiquette classes were mandatory for the social elite, which Astral was entitled to as a result of being the grand-daughter to a member of the Council. However because she was rumoured to be Enhanced, she was also ranked among the servant class. It was the administrations decision to place her in both classes, not knowing if the rumour would follow her into the marriage pool.

Astral's lack of dedication to any of her social obligations often landed her in kitchen duty. What she wasn't aware of was that her teachers in these areas would be the ones to establish her matrimonial price tag when the time came.

"I happened to be away on duty." She folded her arms. That was mostly true. The rest of the time she was napping in the library. "What I'm trying to say is that there's a reason for everything. We don't have as much control of our lives as our masters would have us believe."

"You're sounding paranoid again." Seth smirked.

"I don't think so," she sighed. "You mentioned in your messages that I'd have to put myself on the market when I turn sixteen. What if I don't want to? What if I don't want to get married? What if I don't want children?"

He stared back at her. This was supposed to be her contribution to society. If she married, she'd have two years to reproduce. Failure would have her fulfill her obligations at the war front instead. Breeding was one way to ensure her survival. He couldn't understand why she didn't see that.

"You would prefer being sent into certain death?" Seth asked. It was a fact that only a small percentage of men returned from the war and an even smaller percentage of women.

"It's better than a life of bondage."

"At least it's a life," he snapped.

"You would take freedom of choice over forced servitude," she countered. "You've always talked about making your mark."

"That's different!"

"How?"

"As a man, I don't have the luxury of choice. When I found out about the enlistment, I must have been six years old. I didn't sleep for months. I was plagued by night terrors until eventually I accepted it. I embraced it. I chose to come back alive."

Astral remained quiet, allowing him to speak his piece. She watched the emotions flash across his face. For her, these brief glimpses into his soul were far more revealing than words alone. She saw his childhood terrors. She felt his fear, and finally, his resolve. Astral realized that Seth didn't want to go to war. He wanted to get it over with.

"What will you do when you get back?" She regretted asking such a question. This whole time he had avoiding thinking of the future because he didn't know if he had one. "I'm sorry, don't answer that. It was thoughtless."

They traveled in silence for some time. Seth looked over the documents on his tablet, reading up on the duties that awaited him upon his arrival, while Astral entertained herself watching the wilderness rush by.

They reached the next checkpoint some time later. Under the flickering lights of a deep tunnel, two motorbikes sat waiting. As the car slowed to a stop, Seth spoke. "You can open the package now."

She hesitated before pulling at the plain paper. Inside the box was a long black leather coat. "I rescued it before the Council commandeered your uncle's workshops. I think he meant for you to have it," he said.

Philip opened the door on Seth's side. Seth got out and extended a hand for Astral to take, but without thinking, she had already opened the door on her side and climbed out to try on the coat.

He watched as she pulled it on, and he felt Philip's eyes on him, monitoring his every muscle for a sign of emotional betrayal. Seth cast the bodyguard a casual glance.

"This is the last part of the trip," he informed Astral and gestured to the bikes. "Don't tell your grandfather." He smiled. While travelling separately was dangerous. He had faith in his companion's ability to avoid danger should anything unexpected occur.

She looked to Philip. How did he feel about letting her out of his sight? He nodded, a sign that this leg of the journey would not have occurred if he hadn't approved of it.

They watched as Philip got back into the car and drove off. The driver wouldn't be filing his report to her grandfather until he reached the city, by which time they should be safely behind the capital's shields.

Astral listened to the howling winds. The tunnel was too deep for the wind's reach, but that meant it was also far too long for the safety of the light to protect them. She closed her eyes, allowing her mind to drift.

She felt something nag at her, the familiar sensation of being pulled deeper into a darkness from which she might never return. The tunnel's lights flickered off, leaving them in absolute pitch-black. In that instant, she could see everything that Seth could not.

She saw the demons moving in the darkness, waiting to strike. The sound of the wind had dropped to a low, resonating growl.

Astral gasped as she pulled herself back to the surface of her mind. The lights flickered on, acknowledging her release. She ran her fingers along the underside of the seat, searching for a latch as the tome called to her. She released the latch and pulled the hidden compartment open, revealing the ancient tome nestled inside, humming with anticipation. Astral frowned as she stroke its spine, then closed the compartment.

Seth watched her. It didn't surprise him she found it. What unnerved him was her expression. As her hands hovered over the midsection of the motorbike, he could see her fear. At her age, she had already faced off with more demons than any seasoned veteran of the demon war. Most Hunters of the Red Order would have a hard time keeping up with her record. Yet there was something about this book that struck fear into her.

"We have an opening," he informed her and activated her vehicle using a default start command.

The bike purred in response. "Stay in range." He reached into his pocket and gave her an earbud, then removed his own earpiece.

They exited the tunnel a few minutes later into a heavy snowstorm. The sky had become a deep navy and the force of the wind and snow made the last part of their journey uncomfortable.

Dark, spiralling funnel clouds descended from the sky. "Incoming!" Astral called. The book's power pulsed from beneath her seat, calling to all who would obey.

Seth scanned the horizon. The forest around them was thick, and the demons moved swiftly through its shadows, taking advantage of the impenetrable darkness that the trees provided, but it would thin out as they neared the city. "Keep moving," he ordered.

"It's about to get hairy," she announced just as a funnel cloud touched down a few yards in front of them, forcing the pair to slide to a stop.

It was unlikely that they could outrun the demons, even with the motorbikes. Three more funnels appeared in the sky. "Bet you're wishing that I had a weapon now!" Astral sneered.

"That thing by your right leg isn't decoration," he retorted.

She felt around by her leg for anything that wasn't hot to the touch and would give way with a reasonable amount of force. She gave the cold area a kick, careful not to veer off the road, and reach down to pull the rod free. "If we get separated," Seth said as his weapon shaped itself into existence, "the city is only ten miles up the road."

A demon in mid manifestation lunged from the forest, knocking Astral and her bike off the road.

Its maws chewed at the bike as two spindly legs plunged into the ground to steady itself. Astral pulled herself to her feet, ignoring the pain in her arms and legs. Surface wounds could be treated later. She grabbed her rod from the metal wreckage and activated it, transforming it into a double-sided metal scythe.

She noted that three more demons had manifested to deal with Seth, and two more funnels were bound toward her.

Beside her, the demon continued to gnaw at the bike, crushing it into pieces. As the metal warped and pulled apart, the book slipped out of its hidden compartment. When it hit the ground, Astral felt a shock so strong that it shook her soul, altering her perception of the world.

She stood in darkness. Her weapon was an extension of herself and bore two brilliant blades, so bright they were blinding. She felt her human senses melt away, replaced with something ancient and primitive.

The demon's boney husk was as large as a two-storey building, carried on more than a dozen spindly legs to manage its weight. Its front legs ended in a pair of claws to better rend the flesh from its victims' bodies. The barbs on its tails rattled and spat, splitting into hundreds of hungry mouths as it swayed. It became very clear that this monster was built to kill and feed.

Two eyes burned a dazzling red in the darkness, gazing at her like it had found something entertaining to watch while it ate.

She lunged toward it, one with the demon world, one with the darkness, and severed two of its right legs before catapulting into the air above.

Gravity took hold, granting her enough momentum to plunge her scythe clear through its skull.

She picked up the tome that lay waiting on the ground surrounded by the ruined metal of her motorbike, ignoring the demon's death as it disintegrated behind her. Like before, the book's energy purred in her hands.

"Daamon!" Seth's voice reached her through the earpiece. "Report in!" She could hear him fighting. She struggled to place his voice, like it belonged to some other reality.

A luminescent being ran toward her, fending off a pair of large, swift demons. As his shining blade sliced through them, they vanished exactly as they had formed; in a swirl of dark mist, never to manifest again.

Astral didn't feel threatened by this being. She stared at him in wonder and awe, as though seeing light for the first time. He grabbed her arm, pulling her into his reality. "Daamon!" he barked.

"I'm here," she replied, somewhat uncertain if she was the person he was calling to. The sound of her own voice brought her back. "I'm here," she said again, this time firmly. "I've got the book."

"I've got it covered here," Seth told her. "Run! Run and don't look back!"

Slipping the book under her coat, Astral took his bike and did as she was told.

శుణఖ

She didn't want to leave her friend to fend for himself against such odds. The sheer number of demons that were intent on retrieving the tome made her stomach turn. She hoped that whatever magic pulled them toward it would now draw them away from Seth as their target moved, pursuing her instead.

With three miles left to the capital, Astral spared a quick glance over her shoulder. Sure enough, the funnel clouds were in pursuit, touching down behind her and quickly closing the gap.

She turned back to see William standing in the middle of the road, flagging her down. A row of two dozen masked men in red robes were a few yards behind him, forming a barrier between the surface world and the entrance to the capital. She never thought she'd be happy to see the Red Order.

ಶು 115 ಛ

But she wasn't about to stop until she was beyond the barrier. She sped past William and suddenly she heard nothing at all. Not the eerie stirring of a lurking predator, not the thunderous roars of the veil to the human reality being torn, not even the sound of the Order warding off the demons that were pursuing her.

As she slipped into the tunnel that led to the city, darkness consumed her. She allowed herself a small sigh of relief. The security scanners would verify her identity, while the demon shield beyond would bar entrance to any demons that made it past William and the Red Order.

Astral didn't expect to come to a crashing halt when she hit the demon barrier. The bike slid from underneath her, coming to a stop several feet away and leaving her in a heap at the city's entry point.

She tried to push herself up but only rolled over. The last thing she saw was William's blurred pink face asking if she was all right.

ℴ⚭₿

The sound of a distant drip greeted Astral in her waking moments. She was cold, disorientated, and in pain, sitting in a dark cell, old rusty bars blocking her way to the dim corridor that separated her from other inmates. There were no windows and no other obvious sources of natural light. She tried to recall the sequence of events that led to this moment.

Begging, desperate moans echoed around her. She couldn't see the occupants in the other cells, but she could make out the shape of a man sitting across from her. Something about him wasn't right. He stared at her, unmoving. He could be dead, she reasoned. Somehow that thought made her feel better.

She looked down. Dried blood had stained her coat and matted her hair. The book was no longer on her person. She had failed her mission. Astral couldn't quite figure out how or why she had failed, or why the barriers had barred her entry to the city. She had been to the city before, and yet this time...

"Psst," someone called out to her. "I know who you are," the person cackled. "You shine so bright in here. No, no, don't be afraid. It's okay. You see. It doesn't matter in the slightest. So, you see, don't you?"

She ignored the voice.

"Don't ignore me!" The man in the cell across from hers smashed his face against the bars as though trying to push himself through. The dim lighting revealed just enough of his arms and face to show how disfigured he was: skin had grown over where his eyes once were; blisters oozed a black tar that had hardened all over his body like a bad rash.

"Oh yes, so bright!" he cooed. "Not like the others. Oh no, never like the others. So shiny. Like staring into forever." The man abruptly turned away as though something in his cell was talking to him.

Howls erupted from the other prison occupants. They behaved like wild, hungry animals, banging themselves against the walls and bars of the cell.

The slow thud of heavy boots pounded against the stone floor. A heavyset robed figure strode down the hall. He walked to each cell and lingered there for a short time before moving on to the next.

When the figure reached Astral's cell, he peered into it as though she was an animal on display. She stared up at him, glimpsing sparkling, malicious eyes hidden in the shadows cast by his hood. "For the lady." His voice was raw and crisp. He smiled, revealing a row of sharp teeth, and he pulled out a simple tin cup from his robes.

To avoid revealing her injuries, she didn't move, but the robed figure waited for her to take the offering. Her cellmate turned his head toward the bars. "Go rot," she said.

"No meal for you!" the man hissed and threw the cup and its contents into the cell, splashing its occupants with a thick, red gelatinous substance. A piece of it wriggled on the floor with a life of its own.

Astral watched in horror; she would not be taking any such offering now. The figure laughed at them. "Play nice now," he cackled.

The adjacent occupants cried out mournfully at the lost meal as though Astral had turned down ambrosia.

Once the robed man left, Astral's cellmate regarded her. She wasn't sure exactly how she knew he was looking at her. It was as though the man in the cell with her didn't want to be seen and had somehow willed himself to be a part of the shadows.

"Can you see me, child?" he asked.

She nodded.

"Interesting," he mused. He was silent again for what seemed like hours and in that time he didn't move a muscle.

"Do you see a man or a demon?" he asked at last.

She didn't understand the nature of the question. Why would it matter?

If she was imprisoned with a man, he was long past the point of sanity. If he was a demon, she was in for an interesting sentence. She studied him. "I see a man in demon skin," she said at last.

"Interesting," he repeated. Again, he was quiet for some time, as though the minutes passed differently for him than they did for her.

"Would you like to see if you are right?"

STORY VI
SHADOW PREY
PART II

"Someone turn off that goddamn alarm!" Mallik slammed the empty specimen container onto his desk and collapsed into his chair. He doubted that his voice had carried over the scream of the Council's security alarm.

It wasn't like his staff could do anything about the alarms. At least, not without triggering a secondary system that would reveal his lab existence beneath the capital city's walls – the same walls that kept the demons out.

He glared at the empty specimen container and swiped his desk clean. Another failure. That sample had cost him more than just a few credits.

He watched the rhythm of his lab from the elevated observation deck. The space was wide, housing rows of enclosed workstations. Assistants were carefully pushing research crates between them while other workers swarmed to dismantle the metal and glass frames that created the rounded bubble-like quarantine areas for the experiments.

"All personnel, prepare for evacuation. Sign in projects to your assigned stations before proceeding to the evacuation center," the automated female voice repeated. Her condescending maternal tone grated on Mallik's nerves.

Getting staff to obey the evacuation procedures had taken generations of refinement and the occasional casualty. His great-grandfather modelled the daily doses of information on government propaganda, indoctrinating the workers into a state of fear-based obedience. The lies were simple: the lab is in an isolated location. The world outside is dangerous. See your contract through and everything will be fine. As long as the staff thought they were aiding a return to civilization, they would fall into the routine set out for them.

Mallik tapped his fingers against the surface of his desk. The capital's defence maintenance tests were becoming less predictable, springing into action every few months, sometimes as often as every two weeks. The extra disruptions had a negative impact on his project timeline. His benefactors expected results. Soon.

Another day lost...

His employers weren't after solutions to the demon issue. What they wanted was control over their competition, control over the human threats to their dominion. They wanted weapons to use against each other. Caught up in the stress of exposure, Mallik had forgotten the reasons his ancestors had set up the rigid evacuation protocol to begin with.

The day didn't have to be a complete loss…

He exited through the back of the room.

℠℞

Lights inside the elevator flickered as though tapping out a message. Mallik counted out the rhythm against his leg, waiting for the car to reach the lowest level, a half-mile below ground. As the door to his spartan dwelling slid open, a fleeting shadow dashed down the hall. Such tricks of the light were not uncommon for the exhausted mind. He'd rest… soon, when he finished this batch of tests.

Mallik's accommodations were small, with enough space for a bed and a large workstation. He didn't mind. A lifetime under the Regime's rule made having a room of his own a luxury he was all too grateful for. Having the space to accommodate more than just his bed felt lavish, almost wasteful.

He flung himself onto the chair at his desk and placed both hands, fingers spread, onto the desktop surface. A virtual screen blinked open.

WELCOME DR. MALLIK WRIGHT

A long list of specialized zones allocated to his personal experiments appeared in three columns beneath his name, the same name he shared with his father, who shared his name with his father before him, and so on. No warning signs called for immediate attention.

Even so far underground, Mallik could still pick up the muted screams of the security alarm.

He pulled up the only view of the outside world that he had access to: the capital's entry bay. Years of updates and patches had degraded his family's access to security hardware over time. After a couple of dicey encounters with the city's defence forces, they decided that it was an acceptable loss. It was too risky to adapt to the new software, with its protocols and back-up systems designed to monitor and record everything. Generations of his family had gone through a great deal of trouble to keep their work secret.

The city's tiered entrance came into view; a multi-level, three-mile array of tunnels that allowed everything from trains to small motor vehicles through. Shafts of artificial light marked every ten-foot section. Mallik noted with a pang of jealousy that these lights did not flicker. His labs must be experiencing an energy shortfall. He spoke to the room, "Get a quote on new generators." His personal AI assistant chimed, displaying his request on the new screen in front of him that had popped into existence.

He needed to keep his family's legacy a secret until he had sustainable results, and interacting with the outside world meant a greater risk of discovery. A catastrophic failure with any of the equipment that kept his labs operational, however, would ensure exposure. Best to deal with these issues before they cascaded into something unmanageable. He had the details of a plan should the main system fail. "Schedule routine maintenance," the scientist added as an after thought.

On the first screen, Mallik caught the subtle movement of splintered shadows moving into the entry bay. He guided the view toward the action by touching the digital projection of the area. A group of militarized men, dressed in the white and black uniform of the E.M.I. – an organization of adrenaline junkies who couldn't let go of the war, entered the view marching deeper into the tunnels while using the barrel of their gun to guide the way. A cluster of red-robed figures, Demon Hunters of the Red Order, followed them. Mallik ignored the warning that gnawed at his stomach. He might try to bribe the E.M.I. but if the Red Order were to discover his lab, he wouldn't have the chance to explain the validity of his research. Though he had yet to come into possession of a demon, he knew that the Order's judgement would come down on him. Hard. Generations of research lost to a bunch of half-crazed, self-important, fear-mongering monks.

He pressed his thumb to his lips and watched their slow patrol of the entrance, as they searched between rails and narrow walkways, until they were no longer in view.

A new view finder popped open in front of his active screen.

NEW INDUCTEE REGISTERED.
WARD 1.
FEMALE. HUMAN.
FAILED RESEARCH PARAMETER REQUIREMENTS.
PROCESSING AS SUSTENANCE FOR SUBJECT: WANDERER

Mallik triggered the active camera in the lowest ward, cycling through the night vision feeds of his captives' cells, searching for his ancestor's pet and his new companion. A teenage girl still in a tattered prep-school uniform slumped against the exposed rock of the original compound's walls. He highlighted the insignia over her left breast pocket as another data point for his system.

Was it possible that they were looking for her? Mallik snorted at the idea. It wasn't the first time he'd spirited someone away.

"They're just being thorough in their search," he reassured himself, that is if they were looking for the girl at all.

The previous pop-up relocated in front of Mallik new screen, demanding his attention. Mallik loathe to admit that the annoying perseverance of the AI that monitored his personal experiments helped to keep him on task.

CONNECTION TO THE EXTERNAL NETWORK ACQUIRED.
PROCESSING IDENTIFYING ASSETS.

A close-up of the girl's face appeared on a fourth screen. Mallick repositioned the virtual view, shrinking command screens, while enlarging the monitoring systems of the capitol's entry so that movement would trigger his peripheral vision. He focused in on the girl. Blood drenched the left side of her head, matting her dark hair to the side of her face. A secondary screen related to the AI's search hovered next to the girl's video feed as it ran through the government's registry for girls in her age group, starting with the prep-school she attended: the Council's Academy. His son had graduated from there last year.

MATCH FOUND. RETRIEVING RECORDS.
RECORDS FOR ASTRAL ALEXANDRIA DAAMON DOWNLOADED.
CROSS REFERENCING DATA.

Daamon, why did that name sound familiar? The spelling was unusual too, it should have stood out. Mind you, he couldn't be bothered to learn his staff's names, not with the rate he cycled through them. Who she was didn't matter. She wouldn't have done anything remarkable yet. What mattered now was who would come looking for her. When it came to his acquisitions, Mallik liked to be prepared. He pulled up her family tree.

Damn.

Of the ten million people left on the planet, she was related to the one person who had, on several occasions, nearly ended Mallik's work: Councilman Dezmond Daamon. Normally, a relation to a political figure would have been a boon. In the public eye, their active role in locating their missing child extended no further than the press conferences and media pleas, transforming their child into a martyr for their platform. The loss of one child over six, as per the Council's breeding requirement, was hardly a loss in the grand scheme of things. The power lay in transforming the child into a hero - into a slogan that inspired the politician's constituents.

The half-assed efforts of the search parties meant that Mallik would remain undiscovered, regardless of if he had been involved in the missing person's disappearance.

Dezmond didn't do sloppy search efforts. The first notable difference was that he was appointed instead of elected. He didn't ask for power. He took it.

When Dezmond's son went MIA a decade ago, there was no press conference, no public outcry. The Councilman sent task forces to scour the region where his son had gone missing, imposed inspections on the Red Order monasteries, and raided every level of the capital city. The man had more than power; he had influence. He had come so close to finding his son too...

Mallik smirked. He had outsmarted the man before. Dezmond's thugs hadn't found his labs last time. They wouldn't find them this time. If somehow they did locate his little hideaway, he wouldn't survive the Councilman, but his research might. Was that enough?

The girl would be dead soon. There was nothing he could do about that.

The patrolling unit came back into the surveillance camera's view. They halted. A shadow stretched across the platform in front of them, then shrunk back as Seth entered the frame, wearing the dark uniform of a new E.M.I. recruit.

His son had grown since Mallik had seen him last, but then again, they had rarely crossed paths since the boy announced that he had enrolled himself into the Council's Academy and secured a scholarship. Points of pride for any parent, but for him, it meant losing control of a long-term project and his continuous access to the enzyme Seth produced.

The grey that peppered the nineteen-year-old's hair told Mallik that the boy continued to refuse to take his medication.

On the screen, Seth saluted, thumping his left hand over his heart. The veterans returned the greeting. They had a brief verbal exchange, after which the units looked to one another, shaking their heads. Mallik wished he had audio surveillance of the area.

The lights dimmed and flickered once again, as though a flurry of tiny insects were scratching from the inside of the bulbs. The virtual screen froze, struggling to maintain the connection before blinking out, leaving the scientist with the whine of a system on the verge of failure. Mallik sat back in the dim light, listening to the screeching of the alarm.

A gentle triple knock rapped at the door, and he shuddered in the sudden chill of the room. Turning, he watched the entrance like a child anticipating their nightmare come to life, searching for the signs of feet shuffling beneath the closed door. But it didn't let the light from the outside world in, therefore there was no reason for him to expect to see a presence beyond the room.

This habit from childhood wasn't something he had ever experienced for himself. Yet he remembered the wool scratching his cheeks and nose as he gripped the childhood memento in his small hands with fear. The blanket was blue and white, handmade by a relative. He didn't remember the before or after. He remembered the terror that wasn't his. A residual memory from the original Mallik, perhaps?

The shrill scream of the security alarms might well have been right outside his door. He held his breath, straining to hear the second series of knocks. Would one more dispel the illusion or make it real? The chime that would have signalled the presence of a real person in want of attention didn't sound.

The lights came back to life, washing away the bone-chilling terror with it. "This is just a courtesy," the remnants of his terror echoed deep in his mind, "I'll be coming for you soon."

He gripped the back of his seat, sweating. At some point, he had risen to greet his unknown guest, compelled to answer the knock. Mallik took a deep breath to steady his nerves. "Just a vivid dream," he told himself. He'd been working too hard, sleeping too little. Hallucinations were normal at this stage. He'd end the quarantine as soon as the alarm settled down and schedule some much-needed R&R.

Two weeks. No.

A few days.

Maybe just a day.

He sat down and pulled himself closer to the screens.

The girl's young face wrinkled into a deep frown and she began to make slow, subtle, limited movements, like she was running a checklist of her physical status. She must have been trained for kidnappings. With a guardian like Dezmond, she'd have self-defence training, though her record had shown nothing beyond basic training with the Academy, just enough to qualify her as war fodder.

Her cellmate hadn't moved. Unusual. Though the Wanderer was hard to distinguish even with the night lenses. His soiled, skeletal frame blended too well with the natural elements of the prison. A quick switch to heat sensors revealed nothing that Mallik didn't already know. As far as the camera was concerned, his test subject didn't exist until it moved.

After a decade of starvation, he expected that the Wanderer should have made a quick meal of her. He willed the beast to move, to show signs of life, any sign that it remained in its narrow cell. Nothing. She would have to starve to death instead.

The girl shifted, keeping her movements slight. She rested her head over her shoulder, likely listening for some familiar sound. Mallik tried to remember if the security sirens reached as far as these deep containment wards, but a glance at the erratic pulse of the ward's audio wave showed that the cacophony inside would have drowned them out anyway.

She kept her eyes shut. Not that she'd see anything in the pitch black of her prison. In the deep wards, the lights had stopped working, despite new replacements. His great-great-grandfather had attributed the occurrence to psychic resonance. The inmates of the lower wards had developed a sensitivity to the light that caused their flesh to burn, leaving behind deep scars that never healed.

Mallik kept the feed to the girl's cell open while cycling through the other cells on a separate view. Inmates paced the narrow confines of their prison, torn between the compulsion to flee or attack. They scratched at their deformed heads, trying to reach the itch inside their unravelled minds. Others raged, launching themselves at their security shields. In the glow of burning flesh, bent and broken bars revealed a history of escape attempts.

One inmate pushed its mutilated arm through the shield, grimacing against the pain as the limb blistered and burned. Saliva fell from its malformed jaw, lips pulled so far back that its broken-toothed smile was a permanent feature. It pushed its narrow face between the bars.

The lights flickered. The sound of slowing machinery, struggling for power, distorted the desperate cries of the security alarm above. Mallik's skin crawled. Each zone had its own power supply and his test subjects weren't coordinated enough to create a dangerous shortfall in energy levels, but his confidence did little to undo the knot in his stomach.

Caught between the bent bars and unable to retreat to its cell, the smoldering inmate fell forward, dead. Reaching out, but not for freedom. The exit was the other way, common knowledge for all lifers in Mallik's wards as it was the only direction that the Mongrel emerged from when making its rounds.

The girl's cell was deeper into the ward, but the creature had been reaching in her direction. Mallik watched the electrical current cook the remains until they crumbled into ash, covering decades worth of grime and fluid with yet another layer of death. His shield tech may not have been the top-of-the-line demon prevention technology used to safeguard the city, but it kept hostiles in their cells. He restricted the power to the cell.

Now that he had something to look for, Mallik cycled through the cell feeds a second time. The other inmates, too, fixated on the new guest, butting their heads against the walls of their cage and clawing at their chests. The anticipation of a fresh meal too much for their simple minds.

He needed to get rid of her anyway. Allowing the inmates to feast on the girl would give him some data points. At the very least, he'd relish the secret victory of stealing yet another person from the Daamon legacy.

A resentful quiet fell over the residents of Zone 1 as the Mongrel shuffled into the hall. His flesh oozed a thick, gelatinous compound that was an odd mix of the milky white of infectious puss and crimson-red blood. Though he was human shaped, he looked nothing like the lieutenant he had once been.

He moved with purpose, approaching the first cell. The inmate barked and hissed, voicing its desire for dominance before falling quiet and approaching the shield like a timid pup. A moment passed before the Mongrel pushed a finger through the shield, unflinching. His severed finger fell to the ground. He nodded to the inmate, granting his blessing.

Crude fingers clawed at the filth, searching for the morsel. The inmate pushed the prize into its broken mouth then hissed at its benefactor, who had already moved on. It pressed its head against the bars to peer down the hall. Hunger satiated, it was calmer now, in control.

The Mongrel was the only test subject allowed access to the wards, having proved himself trustworthy – unlike the Wanderer. Mallik remembered the day well that the Mongrel had escaped from his prison. He and his father had searched for the specimen for months. Until one day, they found him, making rounds to each cell, offering pieces of himself until he had nothing left to give. What remained shuffled off to his hiding place in a ventilation shaft where he regrew himself. When Mallik discovered where the Mongrel had made his home, he installed cameras inside and out to observe the rare anomaly that his father had created, and that he had yet to recreate. The Mongrel never made a bid for freedom. Perhaps he knew that it was an impossible feat.

In Zone 1, the Mongrel continued on his rounds, reaching the girl's cell near the end of the hall. He lingered, staring into her cage as though contemplating. The girl didn't react to the figure staring at her. It was possible she didn't see the monster, but she must have heard him. Mallik glanced at the sound level indicator, still pulsing erratically. Maybe not. He was certain that she must have seen something in the electrical light show provided by her self-mutilating inmates.

The shadows in her cell shuddered as though taking its first waking breath from a long slumber. The Wanderer was still alive. Good. The Mongrel jumped back, escaping the invisible reach of the shadow fiend, and swayed with indecision, animal instincts no doubt demanding to assert its dominance over a resisting foe. If the Mongrel made a sound, it was impossible to distinguish his call from the others. The Mongrel threw himself at the shield, but moved in such a way that his gelatinous flesh spattered over the girl and her cellmate, bathing them with his infectious wrath.

The girl rose to her feet in mild annoyance and wiped the waste from her soiled clothing. Mallik wondered if she could stomach her injuries long enough to make a run for it. Fight or flight was hard-wired into the human condition, and it was obvious she didn't have the strength necessary to fight and win. Not that running would save her.

She stood her ground. An interesting choice. A foolish choice, but an interesting one to make while surrounded by creatures hungry for her soft body.

₧ℂ₹

The growing number of Hunters gathering in the city's entry bay drew Mallik's attention.

He scowled at the soldiers, guns held across their chest as they surveyed the exit. Why hadn't they moved on by now? A few feet away lay the first of many invisible demon barriers. That must mean they were regrouping and formulating a new plan. Despite the logical explanation for their actions, their unwillingness to move on bothered him.

The E.M.I.'s commanding officer shouted at the leader of the Red Order pack. Lately, the E.M.I. had been overstepping into Hunter territory, often shadowing Hunter missions. Their ambitions hadn't gone unnoticed, which led to the increased tension between the Council and the Order over tribute and territory shares. The people were losing faith. Too many cities lost. Too many loved ones killed. And now, the demons were knocking on the final haven known to man.

The Red Order needed to prove themselves now more than ever. There was a time when they would have sent a single Hunter to investigate a demonic incident. Today, they sent thirty Master Hunters and apprentices. The E.M.I. was outnumbered three to one. A screaming match would get them nowhere. Mallik wondered if he could prey on their paranoia to fund the more specialized areas of his research. He doubted he could share the depths of his legacy's findings, but he was sure he could find a sweet spot that appealed to the right buyer.

Seth had stepped away from the shouting match with a hand pressed to his ear, listening. He squinted into the darkness, trying to decrypt the fractured message. The shield tech often interfered with communication devices if they weren't routed through the appropriate boosters. He pulled the audio device from his ear and peered down the road behind them, then back down the tunnel that led to the city. He turned, said something to those willing to listen. Soldiers and Hunters squinted at the boy, revealing their displeasure at having had their ignorance challenged.

The leader of the E.M.I. squad cocked his head in serious consideration. A few silent words in response prompted the boy to speak again, at which the soldiers perked up, while the Red Order stiffened at the implications of whatever Seth had proposed. Mallik growled at his screen.

The boy held up two fingers and made his request, to which his commanding officer obliged with a nod. Seth left the entry bay with two soldiers, followed closely by two Hunters at the command of their leader.

Whatever the boy had suggested, it made the Red Order insecure.

The soldiers resumed their patrol, searching shadows and hard to reach places with the barrels of their guns.

He shifted his attention back to the girl speaking with the Wanderer. The Mongrel had made his way from the deep wards as a remnant of his former self, oozing his way toward his nest where he would regenerate himself. The inmates were no longer flinging themselves into the bars. Now fed, they paced their cells, all the while observing the girl in the darkness.

The Wanderer stepped toward the girl, a solid, dark shape against shadows.

She crouched down, plucked an object from the ground and, without inspecting what was most likely the remains of her cellmate's meal, tossed it toward the bars.

Mallik resented having to use such a primitive solution to contain his hybrids. He preferred the city's barrier system, which restricted access to certain sectors based on each citizen's implant data. All of his employees had custom chipped implants, and it made depositing a new test subject to the containment area easy.

But glass or metal slates proved insufficient when the new hybrid's strength grew and they could smash their way through walls with enough time and patience. The first Mallik had made the fortunate discovery of using electrical currents to keep their designer monsters at bay. Pain was pain – it didn't matter the species.

The girl scratched at her head wound, pulling away the scab as she considered her situation. She peered down the hall, counting the numbers of cells as far as she could see on bloodied fingertips. She shrugged when she reached her conclusion. Mallik snarled at the way she dismissed his pets.

The ward's captives sniffed at the air, tantalized by the scent of fresh blood, and the Wanderer watched the girl with expert self-control as the citizens of the deep ward renewed their hunger-driven frenzy. Mallik noted a measure of control in their movements this time. They had stopped driving themselves against their cage, opting for war cries and chest beating, their intentions of consuming the girl announced and then challenged by their fellow inmates.

Blood dripped down her face. She gestured for the beast in her cage to come forward, and when it obliged, she took the beast's elongated hand in hers and placed it onto her wound.

Something about this situation wasn't right.

The Wanderer's ten-foot-tall, skeletal shape towered over the girl as she drenched his second hand with her blood. With both hands covered, she nodded toward the bars and offered a few words.

He drifted over to them, curling his long, slender claws as he seemed to consider the consequences of her request. Then he wrapped his hands around the bars and smeared her blood down them, enduring the pain.

Devoid of shadows, the Wanderer's frail frame appeared brittle and aged. His arms, covered by an extra-thin membrane of leathery, pale flesh that stretched to his hands, now visible. Burns marred the side of the monster's face. But the girl didn't react to his deformities, to the way his nose lay flat to his skull, or his lack of mouth, eyes, or ears, which had been lost in an incident before Mallik took control.

Job done, the Wanderer retreated to the back of the cell where he cradled his burning hands, mimicking the human gesture of blowing on its wounds to cool the burns as it rocked itself. A residual memory of his former human condition.

The girl stood at the bars and made eye contact with the creature in the cell across from her. She gestured toward the bars, pretending to grab them, took a few deep breaths, then mimed pulling them apart. She repeated the action three more times to a growing audience of interested captives.

Mallik had over fifty containment zones nested beneath the city walls A single one housed two hundred creatures in groups of twenty wards. Any more in an enclosed group led to rapid growth of intelligence. Not that they were smarter in larger numbers; it's that they learned faster as their numbers increased. If one learned a lesson, they all learned the lesson. Mallik's great-grandfather had theorized that the cluster shared a telepathic link through visual contact – a hive mind. Even in a hive, there was always a queen... an alpha.

The inmates huffed, snarling at their cage to prepare themselves for the pain to come. One by one, they gripped the bars.

The girl pulled off her long winter coat and covered her crouched cellmate with it, tying her sleeves around its head to secure it in place as some crude turban. With hurried words, she walked him through the steps of a plan.

Would he help her? Mallik hoped not. Things in Zone 1 were getting out of hand, fast. It was fascinating in that it was something different from the status quo, giving him some new data points to analyze. A pang of guilt gnawed at him, reminding him of the legacy he was at risk of sacrificing.

The bars were bending…

There was nothing he could do to save the oldest of his family's creations from the Wanderer once freed.

Mallik's AI assistant announced, "Energy shortage imminent. Accessing back-up generators."

He cycled through the video feeds for each of the twenty wards contained within this zone. They were fighting the currents simultaneously. This wasn't possible. He'd never seen anything like this before; his entire collection operating on the same directive. How would they have received the instruction to break free, now, of all times?

The mechanical whirring of machines and ventilators slowed then stopped and the lights went out, leaving the scientist in darkness.

೮)ଔ

Mallik stared at the space above his desk, his mind struggling to find the logical next step to correct this undesirable sequence of events. It didn't matter, he told himself, in case of complete energy failure, the zone was designed to seal the wards contained within it. They had nowhere to run.

But the measure of control the girl exhibited over the inmates was fascinating.

Mallik beat a rhythm against his desk. Alexandra Daamon, the first daughter born to Dezmond Daamon, had been interested in developing genetically enhanced biological weapons designed to kill demons. That interest led to Seth and his lab-born autoimmune disease. After her death, Mallik had stolen all of her research and eliminated all the project's assets. It was a short-sighted move to be sure, but it meant that he didn't have competition. If the unique enzyme produced as a result of Seth's autoimmune disease proved to be a successful counter agent to demonic infections, Mallik would have the only viable solution to the demon problem – a living, breathing vaccine. Though it seemed that the records he stole were incomplete, as he had yet to recreate a second successful prototype.

Was this girl a different branch of a working prototype like Seth? His heart raced. The implications were severe. If he was right, then Dezmond must have sanctioned the continuation of Alexandra's research. That would make the girl a weapon – Dezmond's weapon – sent to purge Mallik's labs. Which meant that E.M.I. was looking for the entrance to his labs, and explained why they were being so thorough in their inspection of the entrance hub. That meant that the Red Order was present as part of a joint effort between the two factions. It would account for their numbers: enough Hunters to purge centuries worth of monsters. Would they even know the difference between evolution and a demon? Science and black magic?

The machines groaned awake, returning life to the lab. How many systems had been affected by the shortfall? He ran a check. His main labs remained unaffected. The wards, however...

The inmates had broken free and in their frenzy began to cannibalize each other. Meat, blood, bone, nothing went to waste. They barked, hissed, and swiped at one another between large mouthfuls of flesh, attempting to take out any competition for food. They ate with the hunger of starved men. A reasonable reaction since their bodies demanded high quantities of animal protein to maintain their strength. Their growing physical power was one reason he starved them for such long periods. Most would grow frail within two weeks, though older specimens, such as the Wanderer, were starved for years with little to no effect.

Mallik pinched the bridge of his nose. "Flood all wards with neurotoxin," he decided. The bulk of his test subjects would survive the shock, but he'd lose those created in the past year. The girl... well, he'd dissect her and extract her genetic secrets. He'd prefer her alive, but he'd take what he could get.

The lower ward was fully lit and empty. The bars to the girl's shared cell were mangled. Ash, blood, and filth caked the walls. Deep claw marks had damaged the stone. The doors to the ward were pried apart, one layer at a time. Proof of escape.

Mallik switched the feed to survey the adjoining hall. The rows of doors leading to other clusters were bent, revealing deep gouges and bulges in the metal where trapped inmates were forcing their way through.

He went back through the wards. His pets were not succumbing to the toxins as they had so many times before. The inmates had abandoned their meals, allowing them to perish from their wounds and crumble into piles of fine ash. A new data point – they preferred to feed off the living.

The Wanderer's attention steered away from the girl toward the cacophony of the escaping specimens from nearby wards. The girl glanced at her companion as though it had said something, nodded and hurried along a path of dried ooze toward the door. A futile plan if she thought it would lead her anywhere other than the Mongrel's nest.

She pressed her hand to the scanner at the door. Nothing. Mallik smirked, what did she think would happen? Eyes shut, she leaned her head against the multi-layered steel barrier that barred her path.

An eerie silence permeated through the ward. Befuddled, the inmates searched for the source of psychic power. The Wanderer turned and stared down at the girl as though seeing her for the first time. He approached her with caution, claws spread out, ready to slice through her. His movements reminded Mallik of someone preparing to crush a hornet without provoking it.

A glacial cold washed through Mallik's room. His screens flickered. Desperate pounding thudded against his door, giving the impression of hundreds of people outside, begging for entry. The noise spread to the ceiling and walls. He felt the knocking vibrating beneath his feet. Visions of all the people who had died through his experiments became his reality. The souls he had damned didn't want revenge. They wanted him to join them.

He couldn't stay here. They'd find him here.

The cold melted away, washing away the noise. Mallik stared at the door to his room, hand hovering over the button that would have let the monsters in. His mouth was dry, his breathing heavy. He just needed to get some rest, he thought to himself, but found his certainty lacking.

Movement on one of the screens called for his attention.

With the aid of one of his teammates, Seth had returned carrying a wounded comrade. He lay the soldier down on the pathway and felt for the man's pulse. A nod signalled that the soldier was still alive.

Moving the man was the worst thing Seth could have done for him.

The rapid fluctuation of colours of red and yellow told the scientist that two re-purposed automatons were making their way to the dying soldier intending to retrieve him. Seth knew…

As a boy, Seth was familiar with the old ghost stories of people going missing when they had to venture to the surface world, outside of the safety of capitol city which was nestled deep underground. Mallik had tried to squash any interest he might have in such things – if Seth was going to take over Mallik's legacy, he needed to have a practical mind – but Seth had soon learned the truth.

In the early settlement days, the city set up scanners to search for survivors. The automatons looked for wounded, intending to keep humanity's numbers high by any means possible. If they drew breath, they were worth saving. When the city closed itself off from the outside world, demanding registrations and permits to gain entry, the systems were forgotten. All Mallik's ancestor had to do was alter the home destination for the salvaged automatons and devise a restrictive path for them to travel. From that point onward, he had all of the test subjects he would ever need.

At the entry bay, the four-foot-tall glorified vacuum cleaners slid a gurney under the dying soldier. With a cheerful tone, they informed the party that they would lift the man and deposit him at the nearest hospital, whose name only existed in old records. Mallik had heard the automatons' greeting card hundreds of times before.

While he could change the final destination, the automatons had already triggered the path to his lab, meaning that they would return home before rerouting to the new location. There was another option…

Mallik killed the connection to his subject collection system and paused the emergency response system, ensuring that no other automatons were dispatched to collect the wounded.

The automatons' whirling lights faded as they slid to a stop, having already begun making their way home with the dying soldier carried between them. Seth watched with neither disappointment nor frustration. Mallik recognized that expression. Hypothesize, assess, collect data, reassess, form a new theory based on what he had learned. Steps that Mallik had drilled into the boy since he was old enough to ask questions.

Seth marched over and set to work dismantling one automaton's mismatched casing. He pulled diagnostic plugs from its exposed chest and plugged it into his multi-tool, a common practice to locate technical maintenance issues with the machines. Mallik glared at the boy.

Move on.

Diagnostics complete, Seth withdrew his tool from the machine and disappeared out of view of the camera while reading the data. His comrades watched with interest. Mallik's chest tightened, threatening to crush his heart. Seth, he could deal with. A whole army…

The boy's unit followed him off screen. Moments later, a representative from each faction ran toward their respective leaders, who were patrolling far past Mallik's sight.

Time crawled. Mallik would learn how bad the situation was in a few minutes. He didn't dare glance at the mayhem of Zone 1. His mind could only handle the intense stress of one issue at a time. The girl, he could overwhelm and kill, assuming the Wanderer hasn't done so already. But fighting off two groups of warriors in addition to containing the Wanderer and the girl separately… It was all too much! He'd have to choose.

The leaders rushed past Mallik's view of the entry bay. Mallik's instincts told him that Seth had found a viable entrance to his labs through the automaton hatch. It was a tight squeeze at four feet by four feet, but given enough time, they'd get through.

It was possible they'd explore the crawl space as a unit, in which case he could eliminate the immediate threat by killing them one by one as they emerged from the hatch. But if one soldier stayed behind to tell the others…

He couldn't risk it. He needed to leave.

ℰℭ

It was odd how pragmatically Mallik's mind worked once he admitted defeat.

Activate cameras to record.

Download feed to a proxy site within the city.

Encrypt data.

Send feed to broadcast via an encrypted network, embedding a frame every ninety frames for retrieval later.

He would access the network from a safe location and decrypt the transmission later.

Time to decide what to do about the escapees. The girl was interesting enough to have won her life, at least for now. He'd like to keep the Wanderer as a matter of principle. His family had kept him for so long that leaving him felt wrong. However, it wasn't like they had learned any new information from the monster in decades. The Wanderer was disposable.

What about the Mongrel? As long as he didn't leave his nest during the invasion, he might survive. Mallik could retrieve him later. His flesh might be the key to the psychic connection between the wards. It was a long shot, as far as theories go, but there were a series of tests he could explore after the Mongrel exhausted himself.

He cycled through the deep ward feeds, searching for the girl and the Wanderer. In the struggling light, the beast was fighting off other inmates, barring their path to the girl. The Wanderer had changed priorities in the short time Mallik was distracted.

The girl had her back to the fight, putting too much trust in a monster to defend her. The metal doors slid open as the remains of the Mongrel appeared as though summoned. In a swift motion, she captured the Mongrel and held his squirming, gelatinous form at arm's length.

When the light returned to full strength, she smeared her captive against the hand scanner, triggering the door to open. The Mongrel's ability to override the gates to feed the denizens of the wards was another anomaly attributed to psychic resonance. Since the creature had never made a bid for freedom and didn't attack or free the inmates, Mallik had seen no reason to fix the issue.

The girl opened the door to each ward from the inside of the Zone 1 corridor by smearing the Mongrel across the corresponding scanners. He sputtered and spat, swiping at her with stubby claws, until she struck the back of his head and reprimanded him. The Mongrel held its breath and bubbled its fury at her.

If Mallik left things to proceed as they were, he'd lose his family's legacy. He might as well lose everything on his own terms and gain a few new data points while he was at it. He unlocked the path leading to the girl and her protector, all wards in all zones were free to hunt her down. It was unlikely that the girl would survive the onslaught. He doubted that even the Wanderer would survive all five thousand inmates.

The light in the lower ward went out without flickering.

As for him…

He couldn't stick around. It wouldn't be long before his pets worked their way to the main labs.

He released his staff from their evacuation pods – he didn't need survivors leaking the details of his work to competitors – and they meandered from their holdings, finishing conversations with members of their pod. Panic stirred among them when they realized that the alarms were still blaring.

One last thing…

Mallik loaded the kill switch to his lab – the final blow that meant the end to the first Mallik's work. He ran through his options one last time. He authorized the kill command.

By the time Mallik was in the elevator, making his way to the main lab, the internal system had flushed a third of its data. In a few more minutes, the servers would overload and catch fire. The fire may or may not spread to the rest of the facility, but the important part was that Dezmond would not get his family's research.

As Mallik stormed through the labs, his worried staff straightened at the sight of him. He cleared his throat: "Get a team down to sector D and sort out that alarm. I'm fed up with these damn drills. If demons wanted to come this far north, we wouldn't be standing around talking about it." A murmur drifted over the workers. "Get on with it, we have deadlines to meet and I have stakeholders to impress! I had better have something to report by the time I get to my meeting!"

Banging warped the inner wall of the labs. Stifled screams escaped from his staff. Mallik had hoped that he would make it to his pod before his creations surfaced. The wall fissured and several dark, stained human hands pushed their way through, reaching for the light. Mallik swallowed his scream and stumbled backward. They had come for him.

The herd of lab workers bolted, scattering in every direction, forgetting the safety of the evacuation pods. Mallik pushed himself against a wall to avoid being trampled. Monsters, the likes of which he had never seen, leaped from the wall onto the retreating staff. Some scurried upward and dangled from the ceiling, elongated arms plucking up their struggling prey mid-escape. They moved too fast.

Bipedal beasts held screaming assistants down with a single claw, impaling them to the ground and tearing away large chunks of their flesh as though biting into chicken legs.

A string of ceiling monsters sucked on a single long intestine as they passed organs on to newcomers. They were sharing in their feast...

Mallik kept his back to the wall, inching down it, hoping that he wouldn't draw their attention. He found that he couldn't watch them. Instead, he stared at the next few steps of clear wall ahead of him. He could feel the monsters' eyes on him.

These were nothing like the creatures he kept in the depths of his labs. They were intelligent, curious, and calculating. They were toying with him.

If he looked back, they'd pounce on him.

The sliding doors to the evacuation area struck a corpse that was severed from groin to shoulder and slid open a few feet before trying to close again. Bodies littered the adjoining room. He caught a blur moving from one side to the next, a creature launching itself toward a group of escapees, followed by a scream. Mallik was sure that sound hadn't emerged from a human throat. "This way!" he shouted to the dwindling masses. "Quick, to the pods!"

He ran ahead of the herd, hoping that the beasts would take out his staff from behind. Mallik smashed against his pod – the others were fakes, glorified graves to make cleanup easy – and pressed a shaking hand on the scanner to open the door.

He fell into the chamber and collected himself in time to slam on the close button before any undesirables tried to join him. He laughed as he pressed himself against the pod wall.

A deafening, slow screeching sound accompanied a trail of claw marks piercing the door.

Mallik rushed to the console and triggered the evacuation command. He heard the heavy steel door that separated the lab from the outside world come down on the creature. Its scream echoed in his ear. The sound would haunt him until the day he died, of that he was sure.

The pod lurched as it picked up momentum. It would join the rail system soon and attach to the first train heading in his general direction. He was safe.

His deep sobs of relief transformed to laughter. He had survived a demon attack, and what amazing creatures they were. If only there was a way to capture their strength, maybe even bring one of them under his command.

But for now, it was high time he and his son resolved their differences.

CHAPTER 1
AWAKENING: PRODIGY

The staccato rhythm of the artillery units echoed in the darkness of the evacuation center. Parents and children huddled together under the crimson flicker of the emergency lights. A blast reverberated through the secure hold… One less defense unit.

A chorus of cries erupted from those too young to know better. Their call for comfort was deafening. Baleful glares were cast to the parents of the unruly young. Quiet them, lest they be silenced before they call the dark hoards to them. Mothers and fathers pulled their young to their breast, dampening their fear into whimpers while hushing the soothing lullabies that had worked in less dire circumstances.

The refugees of Clearwater dared not voice their rage with the enemy at their doorstep. This time, there are no weapons for the panicked survivors to take matters into their own hands. One disaster averted in favour of another.

Astral, an eight-year-old girl, with long ebony hair sat in a corner watching the survivors succumb to the transformative nature of their circumstance. She watched as friends and neighbours became monsters in human skin.

Her Sunday best was stained and torn, her legs and arms scraped from a nasty fall when the initial stages of panic set-in over Clearwater. She was one of the lucky ones. She cradled her trusty teddy bear between her legs and her chest, keeping her constant companion close, making herself small. Humans were unpredictable in their fear. It was a wise decision to avoid the notice of the strangers with familiar faces.

Somewhere out there, beyond the walls of concrete and steel, her father was fighting a losing battle against the legion of freed demons.

Children fought against their parents' smothering love. Too weak to make any significant impact, their bodies slumped in their parents' hold. Better to pass with love than to suffer the torment of the demonic forces that were bound to take them.

Approving nods with a mix of disdain replaced the hate of the residents of older, well behaved, well controlled, children. In times like these, there was no room for compassion when selfish lives were at stake.

The spark of life drifted from the children, dancing above their parents, confused and frightened. 'Hush now, children, your sacrifice was not in vain.' Astral's moist blue eyes stared up at the void that had been her imaginary friend. 'Why?' her eyes wide, she begged for answers she could not voice.

'Because of you,' her imaginary friend replied. 'Did you think they wouldn't follow? Did you think that choosing a Hunter as your Guardian would change anything?' It was a cruel thing to imply that the razing of Clearwater was the fault of a child. Imbedding the sense of guilt and duty now, during such a formidable time of her identity was crucial. She should not have the option to deny the severity of the threat at hand, nor should she pass her role to lesser hands. The girl had the memories of the time before, a rare condition that most children learn to forget. Not this child. Her memories would serve her well.

The sparkling souls of the children danced around the dark shapeless void, waiting for instruction.

Another blast shook the dust from the ceiling.

"It's not my fault." The child's voice was less than a whisper, her ancient accent still present even after eight years in the new world. Not a whimper in her tone.

"Henry!" a desperate mother cried out, shaking her son's limp body. "Wake up! Somebody help –"

A loud crack silenced her cries as a good Samaritan broke her neck. Her body hit the floor and residents returned to their families.

Silence was the golden rule. All the Council's information channels said so. Don't say a word. Don't breathe. Stay absolutely still. It was all a lie. The demons would sniff them out.

Another blast signaled Clearwater's losing battle. The machinegun fire stopped.

Astral tasted the subtle change of fear to despair. Fear was an acquired taste, but she couldn't stand despair, with a few exceptions.

Ash danced down from the ceiling like snow and the pungent scent of blood and feces overtook the room. Cracks formed on the concrete walls. The lights flickered out. It wouldn't be long now.

Glass shattered against the steel shutters. The deep wallowing howl of the Zephyr called out, and pure silence fell onto the evacuation center.

These people were lost.

The steel shutters resisted the onslaught once, twice, bending and warping a little more with each thunderous attack.

'Daddy's not coming.' The child stood up, her loyal teddy bear in her grip. Breath held, she moved through the refugees toward the shower of broken glass. No-one dared stop her.

'Do it like I told you,' her imaginary friend pulled the souls of the young with her, trailing after the child. Her pulse filled the room as she allowed her senses to wash over the people. Oh no, she most certainly did not care for their flavour at all. Astral's racing heart pounded as she watched the metal twist above them.

'Breathe slowly. Use their fear to guide you. Anchor your purpose within them.'

Astral's breath was short and hollow. Her heart threatened to burst under the pressure. The child's unnatural hold over the people was slipping.

Black ooze trickled into the center, pushing its way through the cracks in the concrete wall expanding the small openings into fissures. It flooded the room, herding the flock of refugees to the heart of their tomb.

The ooze pushed its way toward the cowering residents. It pulled itself upright like a living mass before diving onto the townsfolk and the bold child who stood against it.

'I'm sorry' the imaginary friend told the child before pouring itself into her tiny frame. The transition was painful. Ten years was a short time to forget the everyday aches of the physical world. Time stretched out in all directions forming a nebula of twilight. Past and future versions of Astral approached the child. She had forgotten what it was like to be four feet tall. She had forgotten how imposing she had been as an adult.

The voices of her many incarnations filled her mind, sharing multiple lifetimes of knowledge all stemming from this moment. The best course of action mapped itself out for her and the versions of herself blinked out of existence, save for the masked one which stood at the greatest distance, swathed in shadows worn like a cloak. This one traced a symbol in the air and nodded with the grace of a god.

"They are MINE!" she roared to the darkness, her consciousness returning to the present. The ooze fell back, pushed away by the raw energy the child unleashed.

She shook the dizziness from her head. She felt the original soul of her Vessel fighting her hold. It was strong. Good.

The metal sheet tore from the building, revealing thick dark clouds circling the sky above. The refugees had vanished from the center denying their original existence. "You want them!" The child pounded her chest. A savage smile spread across her face. She jutted her chin toward her target. "They're in here come and get them!"

The ooze rushed toward the child, rose over her and blanketed her in its hate. The ooze turned hot, boiling with fury. Inside it plunged hundreds of needled into her small body, where it formed new threads filling her veins and forced the meat from her bones, working to consume her. She would be made to suffer for as long as her body could withstand death.

It drove deep into her, searching for the taste it craved. The ooze paused in its assault, realizing too late what it had tasted. It recoiled violently, releasing the child from its hold, leaving her in a clear ten-foot vortex of open space devoid of its wicked presence.

Like a second skin, the souls of the last vestiges of Clearwater sparkled over her small form, reshaping her. The luminescent glow of her stigma-infected gaze betrayed her unnatural origin.

The ooze's fluid mass solidified in seconds, poisoned by the soul it had tasted. It shattered and fell to the ground as a heap of black sand.

Howls as deep as insanity, long and mournful, filled the broken center. Black sand danced around the child. The fight for Clearwater was far from over and her time was limited.

ENJOY THIS BOOK?
You can make a big diffence

Reviews are the most powerful tools in my arsenal when it comes to getting attention for my books. Much as I'd like to, I don't have the financial muscle of a New York publisher. I can't take out full page ads in the newspaper or put posters out on the subway.

But I do have something much more powerful and effective. That's you!

Honest focused reviews of my books help bring them to the attention of other readers who may like the same books you do. By being honest in your review, readers can pick out the details they may enjoy. Let's face it, world building isn't for everyone and some readers absolutely need their dash of romance. It's a good idea to tell other readers what this book is and what it is not.

I would be very greatful if you could spend just five minutes leaving a review (it can be as short as you like) on any of the following platforms found through this link: https://bit.ly/2WoFdcK

Thank you very much!

GET EXCLUSIVE AWAKENING MATERIAL

Engaging with my readers has been by far some of the best experiences I've had with my readership. I've learned to tell better stories because of my readers diverse perspectives. In my newsletters, I love talking craft, process, and offer exclusive behind the scenes content that I may not share anywhere else. I also occassionally email with details on new releases, special offers and other bits of news relating to the Awakening and Awakening Fractured Memories series.

If you sign up to the Awakening mailing list I'll send you a copy of some amazing character profiles with professional artwork of Astral, Seth, and William. Exclusive to my mailing list - you can't get this anywhere else.

You can get the character profiles and art, for free, by signing up at http://bit.ly/2MO4hF8

CONNECT WITH A.V. DALCOURT

Amber V. Dalcourt is the author of the Awakening and Fractured Memories series. You can visit the dedicated website over at:
www.awakeninganthology.com

You can connect with Amber on:
Twitter at: @amberdalcourt
Facebook at: https://facebook.com/awakeninganthology/
Pinterest at: https://www.pinterest.ca/avdalcourt/
Bookbub at: https://www.bookbub.com/authors/a-v-dalcourt
Goodreads at: https://www.goodreads.com/AVDalcourt
Discord at: https://discord.gg/7zsemQv

Or you can email her at avdalcourt@awakeninganthology.com if the mood strikes you.